PARTY TRAP

Ross Sutherland was born in Edinburgh in 1979. He is the author of four books of poetry, including *Things To Do Before You Leave Town* (2009) and *Emergency Window* (2012), both published by Penned in the Margins. His theatre credits include *Comedian Dies in the Middle of Joke* and *Stand By For Tape Back-Up*. He also produces the Imaginary Advice podcast.

www.rosssutherland.co.uk

"Sutherland's sheer skill means he's pulled off something unparalleled. It's a proper play, and a proper palindrome, with theme reflected in form reflected in theme."

- TIME OUT

"A daring, virtuosic, valiant failure."

-WHAT'S ON STAGE

also by Ross Sutherland

Things To Do Before You Leave Town
Twelve Nudes
Hyakuretsu Kyaku (e-book)
Emergency Window

First Edition
Published 1.12.16

Published by Imaginary Advice
61 Beluga Close
PE2 8NR
www.rosssutherland.co.uk

Copyright © Ross Sutherland 2016
All Rights Reserved

For more information, contact
RossGordonSutherland@gmail.com

Cover image by Kieran Hood

ISBN 978-1-5262-0642-8

PARTY TRAP

ROSS SUTHERLAND

Introduction

"Did I do sod all lad? O sod, I did."

This is possibly my favourite palindrome of all time. I love the economy of it: simply reverse the question, and you get the answer. You could describe it as a self-answering question. Of course, the majority of rhetorical questions are self-answering. It's just that rather than through implication or innuendo, this one *literally* codes the answer into the question. To decipher it, you just have to shift your perspective. The lock turns into the key.

I also love this palindrome because it's about realising that you've wasted your life. As someone that spends far too long thinking about word puzzles, I relate to this deeply. This is a palindrome about me.

Over the years since I first heard it, I've embellished this palindrome considerably. Now I tend to imagine it as a short story. For sake of melodrama, let's put the speaker on his or her death bed. The speaker calls through to their teenage son. Bedside candles ripple as the youth sits, awaits his final correspondence. After a phlegmatic interlude, the speaker leans in, whispers, "did I... do... sod all, lad?" There is a pause. The son (played by Freddie Fox) leaves a beat of disappointment, then offers a single sarcastic eyebrow. The speaker immediately realises the utter pointlessness of the question, mumbles, "Oh sod. I did." Then promptly dies. The moral: don't waste precious time worrying about wasting time. The answer was right there in the question, stupid.

Keep that sad little scene in mind as I welcome you to this book: my attempt to write an hour-long palindromic play. Every single page of this book might appear to be pleading with you, "Reader, what the fuck am I doing? Have I wasted my life?" But just like the palindrome above, I recommend leaving this question to answer itself. Yes, obviously, this was a waste of time. I lost six months to this story; time I could have spent writing half a dozen other things. Or maybe taken those Spanish lessons like I keep threatening. Yes, this was a waste of time. But all the same, I'd like to mount a defence for wasting time. If living inside a palindrome for half a year has taught me anything, it's that time doesn't just dwindle away. It has a habit of returning to us, in unexpected ways.

I have always been interested in the relationship between language and time. Time moves differently within stories: a thousand years can pass in a single sentence; a car crash can be slowed down to fill an entire novel. Language can double back on itself; moments can repeat. We can revisit the same kiss in a parallel timeline, play out alternate realities. Language lets us time travel, in an analogue crappy kind of way. Though past projects of mine have flirted with this idea, I've never experienced the movement of time in a more profound (or confusing) way than this project. Writing a palindromic drama has reshaped the way I think about time.

Palindromes are closed systems. They always end the same way they begin. With that in mind, we could write the opening palindrome like this:

1. Diag 1

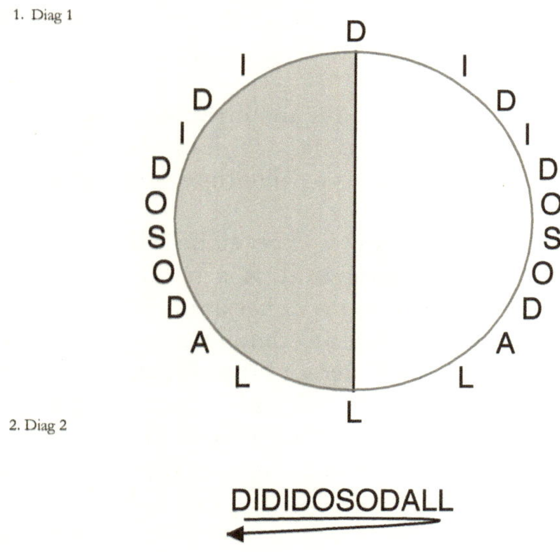

2. Diag 2

DIDIDOSODALL

The first diagram shows a palindrome as an infinite loop, mirroring at both the top and bottom. The second diagram illustrates the same idea, but rather than showing time moving continuously forwards, here the motion is oscillating. Time lurches backwards and forwards, a handcar trapped on the same small piece of track.

None of this matters when observing a single palindromic sentence, but it becomes increasingly relevant when you try to expand the structure further. Faced with writing an entire drama based on palindromic principles, I realised that the world of the story would inevitably be bound by these same laws of time. These characters would be trapped inside a world that could never extend beyond the text of the play. They would be prisoners of symmetry, always ending up in exactly the same place they started. *Party Trap* was therefore designed to be a Möbius strip: a story that continues forever, the text moving forwards and backwards without a clearly defined seam, just as the Möbius strip has no definable 'outside' or 'inside' surface.

3. Möbius strip

For *Party Trap*'s protagonist David Bradley, time has become a sickening loop. He is always a prisoner, even if he doesn't realise it. When the moment comes to start the story over, David willingly sacrifices all that he has learnt in exchange for a brief moment of ignorance, despite the pain and suffering that will inevitably follow. Although not stated explicitly inside the text, it is hard not to imagine that David is trapped inside his own personal Hell. Time is a symbol of mortality, after all. Finding oneself removed from time is therefore intimately associated with death. Hell is eternal, so we're told, full of nightmarish spiral-prisons designed to torture us forever. Sisyphus got the boulder. Ixion got strapped to a flaming wheel that turns *ad infinitum*. Demons never clock-off.

With that in mind, I had initially conceived *Party Trap* as a durational piece. I imagined the play performed several times over, back to back, stretched over the course of an entire day. Certain elements of the story would accumulate over multiple iterations (David would have to lose a different appendage with each new loop). Audiences could enter and leave at any point, further obscuring any linear start and end point of the story.[1] Repeating the loop over and over would also give audiences a chance to get a better grip on the strange syntax of the play, which can feel a little alienating on first encounter. For our opening run at Shoreditch Town

---

[1] Equity probably has rules about trapping actors inside hellish ten-hour time-loops, so maybe fair enough. But I still would like to see this some day.

Hall in October 2016, we had to settle for a single cycle of the story, with just a subtle suggestion of the story continuing again. This version of the script follows the same pattern: we see David briefly begin his next cycle, but then story continues without us.

Whether David is actually dead, comatose or simply dreaming feels unimportant to me. Nevertheless, he is trapped inside a nightmare, that much is certain. The palindromic structure gives everything within *Party Trap* a dream-like quality. The story is always struggling to maintain its palindromic structure, and this struggle shapes every aspect of the journey. The palindrome forces strange behaviour. It breaks reality, generates acts of magic. My hope is that these abnormalities feel expected (perhaps even inevitable). The symmetry provides a rhythm that we onlookers can internalise, anticipate. The strangeness is normalised, just like in a dream. Whenever I am dreaming and my dad appears, I never question why he is dressed as Mr Pringles, or why he is talking about patio doors in such an animated fashion. My dream-self just accepts it. In *Party Trap*, I wanted to use symmetry to try and fake that feeling, helping audiences accept this bizarre story and the weird dream-logic it utilises.

Real life is rarely symmetrical, and yet we idolise symmetry. We judge attractiveness in people based on the symmetry of their faces. We look for it in literature too: the classic myth story structure is a circle.[2] In this way, *Party Trap* is actually a pretty conventional piece of storytelling.

At the same time, I think *Party Trap* inevitably pushes symmetry to such a ridiculous excess that it stops feeling satisfying and becomes nightmarish. Perhaps this stems from our fear of the doppelgänger, or from our utter helplessness in the face of determinism. Symmetry begins to feel inhuman, paralysing. There are no surprises down the road: only the same mistakes, over and over. The narrative arc of a palindrome will always be a parabola: they're prescriptive tragedies. Given the form of the story, you might think it would be obvious that a palindrome would end as it begins, yet somehow it still feels like a horrible trick to play on an audience. To those people that feel cheated, I apologise. There is no way out of this trap.

---

[2] Just like my circular palindrome (diag.1), the classic story circle has a "light half" (representing life, the conscious mind, order) and a "dark half" (representing death, the unconscious, chaos). I think this was inevitably internalised into the structure of *Party Trap*: the reverse side of the palindrome becoming the equivalent to the satanic message in a Judas Priest record.*

* gslft swvzw rxzml mobdz opgsi lftsd zoohg szgdv ivmgg svivd svmrd zhzor evnbb zsllz xxlfm grhki lyzyo bhgro ozxgr evsrg nvfkh lnvgr nv

Party Trap doesn't reverse letter-by-letter, nor does it reverse word-by-word.[3] The play mirrors roughly 'line-by-line'. Some of these lines are complete sentences. More commonly, the line is a sentence fragment. When reversed, the lines reassemble, creating new sentences out of the starts and ends out of their immediate neighbours.

This has a kind-of 'tidal' effect on the storytelling process. Once we reach the half-way point, language starts to retreat backwards, but because everything is reversing in small chunks, the audience can hopefully still recognise phrases from the first half. The second half should feel like one long episode of d*éjà vu*.

It felt foolhardy to approach this project with a solid story already in mind. I liked the vague idea of building the story around the concept of mirrors. Specifically, the way that mirrors lie to us. Both in a literal sense (by flipping the x-axis) and in a more allegorical way. We humans have only ever been able to see the world through reflections. In the last thirty years our mirrors have begun to fracture exponentially. Now there are millions of competing mirrors, all asking us to confuse their reflection with the real. Reflections become further distorted, simplified; new cynical forces emerge to exploit our reality-fatigue. It might be interesting to know that I wrote *Party Trap* during the 2016 UK/European Union Membership referendum, throughout which I regularly heard politicians and journalists on both sides of the debate making exactly the same statement to prove ideologically opposite points. Meaning has seemingly become so fluid that you can reverse an argument simply by repeating it.

The finer details of the story evolved slowly in negotiation with the form. I worked on two documents at the same time: one tracking forwards from the beginning, the other tracking backwards from the end. Eventually, a story began to coalesce: something about the aggressive takeover of a TV programme and the arrest and re-education of its liberal elitist presenter. As Sir David loses control of his programme, he loses control of his image, until eventually his own words get turned against him. All this stuff ended up feeling like a good thematic fit for the form. More than that— it seemed to flow naturally through the form, seemingly writing itself. Other elements crept into the story through the back door. The setting got pushed into the near-future[4]. The politics discussed by the

---

[3] Oh, don't be disappointed. Are you insane? If I committed to either of those approaches, I would have lost my fucking mind.

[4] Making it a genre piece helped sell some of the more allegorical aspects of the story.

characters becomes maddeningly vapid at times (their arguments are often pitched at the level of a Youtube comment section). Balancing the text required me to add a lot of nonsensical TV shows playing in the background. These stylistic aspects certainly make the story more alienating, but they still feel appropriate for the world of *Party Trap*. The story lives in a parallel reality where language has become utterly corrupt. In the Britain of *Party Trap*, meaning can be reversed in a heartbeat. The remaining political conversation is shrill and empty. There's no room for nuance here. It might seem like a heavy-handed pastiche, but real life FOX News doesn't sound that different, really.[5] *Party Trap* gets closer to this reality every day.

*

In January of 2016 I had a near-death experience, collapsing on the floor of a hospital waiting room. I'd been waiting over four hours to be seen about my asthma. The triage nurse told me that I'd just have to wait like everyone else, and I was too British to complain. So I just sat there in the lobby and slowly suffocated. Did I do sod all, lad? O sod I did. Eventually I just keeled over on the tiles. I woke up on a ward later that night, hooked up to a nebuliser, delirious from sucking on the pure oxygen. I had no idea where I was or what had happened to me.

The following day was one of the happiest days of my life. Despite my stubbornness, I had not died. On the bus home, I re-bought The Mountain Goat's album *Tallahassee* as celebration. Falling back in love with John Darnielle's pop masterpiece should have provided this minor episode with the necessary amount of closure, and yet something continues to hang over me. There are rules one is supposed to follow in the aftermath of such things. Near-death experiences are supposed to be recycled into fist-pumping celebrations of survival. We're supposed to carry these moments around with us, hang them around our necks: totems of life, luck, fate, etc. Listen to any religious conversion story or AA confessional. The brush with death is almost always in there, the decisive turning point in our grand narrative: "Whenever I get stuck in traffic, I just remember that ostrich that nearly took my face and, my god, it helps me be thankful for the little things!"

I try to follow these protocols, lifting myself out of shitty moments to reflect on how lucky I am to still be alive. Oh yum these croissants, etc. But rather than feel a lust for life, something else happens. Dwelling on

---

[5] If FOX News turns out to be a twenty year long palindrome then OK everything finally makes sense at last.

that night in the hospital always ends up leading me back to the same insane thought: *what if I actually died that night?* What if everything that has happened to me since is nothing more than a death-bed hallucination? Is this my final dying breath, slowed down to last an entire year? Have my fading memories been shakily translated into future events? Is that why the world seems so recycled, so repetitive? Christ, they've re-made *Porridge*? Now it makes sense. It's just old crap from the back of my brain being repackaged as the present.

Rather than feeling more alive, I am left feeling increasingly dead. But I think the result is equally transformative. These bouts of madness only last a few seconds, but in these moments I feel lifted out of time altogether. I feel as if I am looking out of the window of an aeroplane as it ascends through the cloud cover. It is terrifying, exhilarating. For a moment, time is no longer a draining tap. Time becomes a vast impossible ocean beneath me. There is no such thing as wasted time. Every moment remains.

Apparently, hikers swear on the merits of walking backwards, particularly when climbing hills. It puts a lot less strain on the knees, I'm told. Because walking backwards requires more cognitive control, it also sharpens your senses. Vision is said to improve. Which really is perfect, considering that this way round, you get to see everywhere that you've been; the world expanding with every step.

I wonder if those hikers look at photographs of their expeditions and think: *hang on, was this taken on the way up or on the way back?* In truth, the answer isn't important. Everything you need to know is hidden inside the question.

I think my mountain climbing days are sadly over. The air up there is too thin for me now. Thankfully, there are other types of mountain to climb. Writing this play was my harebrained attempt to capture that feeling: that moment where forward or backwards starts to feel like a meaningless distinction. Even if the play ultimately fails, the intended purpose remains. If only we could find a way to step outside of time, how then could we see ourselves? Surely there are things we can learn from death without dying.

> *Backward Bill, Backward Bill,*
> *He lives way up on Backward Hill,*
> *Which is really a hole in the sandy ground*
> *(But that's a hill turned upside down).*

> *- Shel Silverstein*

Note on the text

The strange broken syntax of the play creates a lot of problems for actors. Whilst writing, I found it useful to imagine *Party Trap* within the conventions of film noir. Like noir, *Party Trap* exists in a fatalistic dream-like world. More importantly though, actors who play noir heroes are usually required to downplay their performance to balance against the expressionistic worlds they inhabit. Sir David Bradley certainly fits the noir hero archetype. Like all noir heroes, he is a walking corpse, wandering through a world that he has already left behind. Hence, the strange broken language of *Party Trap* benefits being 'deadened' in some way. Burying the strangeness of the text seems to keep us within the flow of the story.

I've added quite a lot of annotation to this version of the script. Left bare, some sections of the script felt opaque. These notes might prove useful or incredibly annoying. I've tried to lay out the words in such a way that they will be easy to skip over if deemed boring and/or unhelpful.

I'm imagining two potential types of reader of this book: those here for the story, and those that want to bypass the top deck and head straight down to the palindromic engine room, just to see if I've kept my promise. With that in mind, the book contains two different editions of the script. The first one (Performance Version) is optimised for story, with all the palindromic shuffling hidden from view. The second edition (Pure Text Version) is presented to highlight the palindromic structure.

Thanks to director Rob Watt and to Simon Hepworth and Zara Plessard for all their time and patience on this project. Additional thanks to Jeremy Warmsley for writing the music and to Shoreditch Town Hall and Arts Council England for their support throughout.

RGS 1/11/16

SIR DAVID BRADLEY
Once a respected foreign correspondent, Bradley has spent his twilight years holding down an increasingly farcical role on his political talk-show, *Heart of the Matter*. Massive coronary beckons.

MP AMANDA BARKHAM
Media Secretary for the newly elected 'Freedom Party'.

JEFF HANCOCK*
Producer of *Heart of the Matter*. Longtime friend of David.

ADMIN DESK*
Unnamed civil servant in charge of "professional redevelopment".

* only appears onscreen

PERFORMANCE VERSION

[Pre-set, audience entering]

A desk. Two chairs.

On the desk:
a meal tray; a bowl of cereal with spoon; a glass; a remote control; a
framed photo of a woman.

Sat on the left chair, SIR DAVID BRADLEY (50)
barely conscious, head slung low. He wears an expensive suit.

On his left hand: a missing finger, bandaged.
Blood drips onto the floor.

Filling the back wall, behind Sir David: a video screen.
ONSCREEN: raw static, a droning sound.

[Start]

ONSCREEN: a karaoke video begins.

David numbly rises, microphone in hand.
He sings the karaoke song to the audience.
The lyrics appear on the screen behind him,
scrolling over stock footage of a middle-aged couple falling in love.

As David sings, he thaws.
The song unlocks a forgotten romance: a love lost.

> SIR DAVID (sung)
> My heart dissolves everything…
> that's not what it seems.
>
> —You're all that remains.
> I see you in dreams.
> I see you in dreams,
> I see you in dreams,
> I learnt it all in dreams…
>
> All the clocks struck thirteen;
> I learnt how to survive,
> a guillotine right through my heart.
>
> I taught myself to drive:
> wheels turning in the dark.
> I learnt to live the same.
>
> Nothing ever really dies;
> I learnt that nothing ends…
>
> I had a song in my head
> I learnt a new routine
> I learnt it all in dreams.
>
> My heart dissolves everything
> thats not what it seems…
>
> You're all that remains—
> I see you in dreams (I see you in dreams)
> I see you in dreams (I see you in dreams)
> I see you in dreams (I see you in dreams)
> I learnt it all in dreams…

Song ends.

David tries to wipe a tear with his bandaged hand— winces at the pain.

He looks around to get his bearings.
The stage has become **SIR DAVID'S TOWNHOUSE.**
Of course he is in his house.
Where else would he be at this time in the morning?
Any strange memories fade away.

David slumps back into his chair. Looks at his breakfast. A clock ticks.

David looks at the framed photo of a woman. Beat.
He guiltily drops the photo onto its face.

David begins to eat his breakfast, jabbing his remote control at the screen:

ONSCREEN: TV advert for "Love.com"

> ADVERT
> *Facing the wrong direction?*
> *You just spent your whole life-*

Bleep - he changes the channel. Now a driving school program:

> PROGRAMME
> Voice 1: *There was no turning!*
> Voice 2: *What are you talking about?*
> Voice 1: *How did you even do such a thing?*
> *You managed to turn-*

Bleep - he changes the channel. Now a dubbed French romance. Two
lovers, mid-clinch. (nb. It's from *Les Choses de la Vie*)

> FRENCH FILM
> Male: *….everything against me. Every word I said.*
> *Every threat. Every promise…*
> Female: *You can keep them! They might be worth*
> *something someday…*

ONSCREEN: the couple kiss.

David looks away, love-sick.
He tries to pull himself together.

A lame confidence:

> SIR DAVID
> Maybe it's the re-recorded vocal.
> It… sounds strange. Not as I remember.

Bleep - He changes the channel. Now an advert for a loan company.

> ONSCREEN
> *A loan! It's so easy! Anyone can apply! Their situation-*

Bleep - He changes channel. Back to the "Love.com" advert again.
The backing music on the advert is an instrumental version of the
opening karaoke song.

David listens to the music, lost in reverie.
He looks at the dropped picture frame; props it back up again.

David laughs to himself. He knows it's cheesy but…

> SIR DAVID (talking to picture)
> I do genuinely love this song. I'm not ashamed to say.
> It reminds me…

He stares at the advert, lost inside it for a moment.
A young couple walk on a deserted beach. It looks like heaven.

> SIR DAVID (throat dry)
> …how it feels… to be completely…in love…

Beat. He coughs, laughs, shakes it off. *Come on David, pull yourself together.*

Changes the channel again: Bleep. Takes a mouthful of cereal.

ONSCREEN: an advert for a new season of "Heart of the Matter".
A montage of news events, politicians talking. Dramatic music.

David's face appears onscreen. He's the host of this TV show.

> SIR DAVID (mouth full of cereal)
> Yaah! This! Now this is what I'm talking about.
> You're home old boy-

Overexcited, he chokes on his cereal, coughing the remains back into his
bowl.

TV ADVERT
That's right… He's ready…Sir David Bradley.

David staggers around wheezing, patting himself on the back.

ONSCREEN: a bible advert. Jesus appears onscreen.

BIBLE ADVERT

V/O: *Who is this, "Jesus"?*
Jesus: *It's coming back, already….*
           Everything is coming back…
V/O: *You see? Just take a look at yourself.*
           There's no stopping now!
Jesus: *Let me… help you!*

SIR DAVID (coughing, to screen)

-won't you?

Fit finished, he flops back into his chair, upset at his own stupidity.

ONSCREEN: advert changes to a party political broadcast for the
"Freedom Party". The programme is flashy, edited quickly. It looks like a
CK One advert: full of models and animated text.

David watches it despairingly.

FREEDOM PARTY ADVERT

V/O: *We can trust you to be yourself…*
           to do the right thing.
           But we can't trust you-
           when it comes to a vote.

ONSCREEN: a cross-eyed man shoves his voting slip in a toaster, then
stands beside it grinning.

FREEDOM PARTY ADVERT

Voter: *"I voted!"*

ONSCREEN: caption reads, "Apply to be a Super-Voter today"

Bleep - David changes the channel. Now a sex-line advert: girls dancing.

David takes a cloth from the desk drawer. He starts to mop up the spilt
milk, still holding the remote in his other hand. As he cleans, he gets
increasingly irate at the TV, jabbing the remote aggressively:

PARTY LINE ADVERT

The party is ready to make the call!

Bleep - A home security advert.

HOME SECURITY ADVERT

It's your house. No one can tell you
what to do in your own house-

Bleep - A kids show. Puppets discuss etiquette.

KIDS SHOW

Puppet 1: *Can I go? Say "please!" You did well!*
Puppet 2: *Please!*

Bleep - A programme on the moon landings.

DOCUMENTARY

None of this actually happened-

Bleep - A stairlift advert.

STAIRLIFT ADVERT

…your home a prison?

Bleep - A bathroom advert: a split screen between toothpaste and mouthwash.

MOUTHWASH ADVERT

Which of those two feels more substantial to you? Maybe-

Bleep - A life insurance ad.

David accidentally scrubs his cereal bowl onto the floor. He holds in an expletive- gets on his knees and starts to clean up the mess, remote still in hand. He can't leave the TV alone.

LIFE INSURANCE ADVERT

You came to work, did your job, then came straight home again.
Today was just another day. Before-

Bleep - A vodka advert. A man surrounded by women in bar. Loud music plays.

VODKA ADVERT
Act like any story you like. You get to decide!

Bleep - Another bible advert.

BIBLE ADVERT
You can choose to believe.
Is that what you want to hear? I think you can-

SIR DAVID
I can't.

Bleep - A life insurance ad. An old woman shuffles room to room.

LIFE INSURANCE ADVERT
V/O: *How can you get back all the things you've lost?*
Woman: *"I'm sure there's a way…."*

SIR DAVID
I'm not-

Bleep - A home insurance advert.

As David changes the channel, he tries to stand up, hitting his head on the underside of the desk. He yelps.

HOME INSURANCE ADVERT
A meal on the table… books on the wall…
Your gorgeous townhouse… all nice and warm…

Clutching his head, he turns off the TV, petulantly throwing the remote across the floor. He sits on the floor and sulks. After a beat, he relaxes:

SIR DAVID (to self)
What if… What if you were here…

He looks at the framed picture on the desk above him.

SIR DAVID (to picture)
…in your house. Right now.
I wonder what you would think
if I said we were blessed with a TV
that spews… 99% insurance adverts.
        (beat)
You've got to laugh.

He tries laughing. It sounds awful. He gives up. Rising:

> SIR DAVID (to picture)
> At least the place looks clean. Fixtures are in good nick.

Sits down, wrings his milky cloth into the cereal bowl.

> SIR DAVID (to picture)
> See, I've been working hard. Are you proud of me?

Beat. David looks at the remains of his breakfast, sighs.

> SIR DAVID
> I need…

David retrieves a decanter of scotch. He pours a glass.

> SIR DAVID (quiet, to picture)
> …a drink. No, this isn't the first time I've done this.

He sniffs the whiskey.

> SIR DAVID (quiet, to picture)
> Some days it feels easier than others,
> you might be surprised to learn.

Long beat. David is lost in thought.

> SIR DAVID (to picture)
> I know it wasn't easy in the end. For either of us.
> I wish you could see how things have changed.
> Maybe… when we meet in the next life-

He toasts the picture, slugs his whiskey. Coughs up his lungs.

David retrieves a dictaphone from the desk drawer.
He holds it pensively, looks over at the framed photo:

> SIR DAVID
> This is all for you, you know. It's your fault.

He warms up his vocal chords. Clicks the dictaphone to 'record'.

> SIR DAVID (into dictaphone)
> Mmmmumum. This is…

David's voice breaks. He breaks off, embarrassed.
David tries again to get into character, affecting a smoother, more confident 'TV voice'.

> SIR DAVID (into dictaphone)
> "This is Sir David Bradley, host of Heart of the Matter."

Clicks dictaphone off again. Disgusted at his own smugness:

> SIR DAVID (quiet, to self)
> Oh God. It's so bloody over the top.

He clicks the dictaphone back on. David paces the room, taking audio notes for his autobiography. His 'TV voice' becomes stronger and less affected as the speech continues. The end feels practically sincere:

> SIR DAVID (into dictaphone)
> Start of a new chapter…
> "The cost of disagreeing in the new world
> brings… celebrity. The only real thing you
> have to pay attention to— the sound
> of the free press drowning out the lies!"

ONSCREEN behind David: clippings from newspapers, breaking political scandals. We're seeing the inside of Sir David's ego…

He retrieves a journalism award from his desk drawer, thumbs a smudge.

> SIR DAVID (into dictaphone, re: his award)
> "These shiny little things are just for show.
> Look past them, you'll hear *quality journalism*.
> Press, bright-eyed as ever! Although,
> it's hard not to make jokes when you challenge that
> decrepit old box of farts…"

ONSCREEN: a press clipping with a photo of a past cabinet.

> SIR DAVID (into dictaphone)
> "Once you've unpacked all their lies…
> Shit… sometimes it makes you laugh."

He puts his award back in the drawer.

> SIR DAVID (into dictaphone)
> "You know, I'm so high that sometimes
> I forget journalism is a grassroots thing…
> is part of… being on this planet …is the right
> to ingest *all* the available information,
> reaching a rational conclusion."

Gaining confidence now:

> SIR DAVID (into dictaphone)
> "And sure… I'm smoking hot as I do it.
> That's my style! I confess: I don't give a shit
> about pop stars, dogs in sitcoms, whatever muppet
> floats through the internet on any given morning…
> my hands are full with the important stuff:
> sexing up statistics, dubious spending,
> criminal mismanagement. That's what *I'm* talking about…
> As a journalist, I don't care about the consequences.
> We will not be intimidated, trust me.
> You don't know what this party is capable of?
> Direct that anger towards us… and we will show you.
> *The right people at the right time,* that's us."

ONSCREEN behind Sir David: animated news graphs. A white column
(labelled "Freedom") grows, dwarfing all other parties. Footage cuts to a
celebration, balloons falling from ceiling. Caption: "Landslide Victory for
New Freedom Party".

> SIR DAVID (into dictaphone)
> "The political system has finally been overthrown by…
> joyless excrement tunnels… who want Britain
> on the receiving end of their easily manipulated
> pronouncements. Determined to terrify the public!
> Massive spanners! Look at them!"

ONSCREEN: some very young politicians entering 10 Downing Street:
attractive, dark colours. Caption: "Freedom Party Take Office".
David mocks them as they pass the camera:

> SIR DAVID (into dictaphone)
> "All these reactionary, cum-stained men who love
> to pleasure themselves with doctored photographs
> of burning cities…financed by amateur hypnotists…
> …<u>This</u> deranged homeless-kicking pornographer.
> …A terrifying illiterate baby!"

David retrieves his flung remote control. He rallies for the end of his stump speech:

>   SIR DAVID (into dictaphone)
> "Behind every injustice, there is always a journalist,
> exposing the truth. No need to thank me.
> You want to know what's real? This! (gestures to his heart)
> This is our job! That's why we're here! To help you…"

Sir David flags. It's all too stupid. Massive decline in energy…

>   SIR DAVID (into dictaphone)
> "…see the world as it really is." Meh.

He turns off the dictaphone. All his confidence has drained away. He can't sustain it any longer. David sits and stares at the screen, exhausted.

ONSCREEN: more news articles about the Freedom Party.
Caption: "Record Breaking Turnout For New Party".

He puts the dictaphone back in its drawer. His eyes catch the framed picture on his desk.

>   SIR DAVID (to picture)
> Yes. Times are changing. You never know what's coming.
> I must say… they've got better at fighting back.

ONSCREEN: a more recent newsreel: "Government Declares Ban on Press Communication Until Further Notice" ; "Media Blackout? New Regulations to be Announced."

>   SIR DAVID (to picture, re: news)
> Then we have this… a clever tool introduced by our
> new government. As you might imagine….
> it's got harder to hold people to standards.
> Especially when they refuse to engage with you at all.
> It's sad. Pathetic really.

ONSCREEN: footage of the door of 10 Downing Street. No one going in, no one coming out.

>   SIR DAVID (to picture, re: news)
> You can't see what's really going on the other side!

Back on his feet now. He barks at the screen, frustrated:

                    SIR DAVID
          Come out! Just walk through a door!
          Like, it's the easiest thing in the world! You think you can?
          As day follows night, lightning signals thunder…
          You and me, we're supposed to work together!
                    (turning away, then turning back-)
          You act as if you don't get it- I know you do!
          …Fuck it—

Sits, checks his reflection in his cereal spoon.

                    SIR DAVID
          I see… one tired son of a bitch. Jesus.

Drops his spoon, grabs the remote again. David quickly cycles through
the channels. Endless bad adverts strobe past:

                    SIR DAVID
          I see nothing bad, I see nothing good… I see…

ONSCREEN: another Freedom Party political broadcast. More flashy
images, trendy music. A montage of young MPs posing like catwalk
models. A water-skiing hunk, captioned "Donald Montague, Treasurer".

                    SIR DAVID (sighs, exhausted)
          Fucking… punks. What is going on, my god.
          You really want them to suffer.

ONSCREEN: the caption, "Now broadcasting on our own TV channel.
No more media bias!"

                    SIR DAVID
          Hm. Little clue.

David gets up to clear the table.

ONSCREEN behind him: "Breaking News". He turns back:

                    SIR DAVID
          -What's this-

ONSCREEN: a muted news report: "Politicians to be Protected Under
New Hate Speech Laws" ; "Verbal Assault Could Carry Prison Sentence".
Next, a subtitled interview with Freedom MP Amanda Barkham: "MPs
are vulnerable. They need to be protected…"

David laughs weakly.

                    SIR DAVID
          Oh no. This is too much. Oh, please.

Surely they can't actually do this? David's amusement trembles. If true,
this could be very bad for the show… It must be a hoax of some kind; a
publicity stunt to divert attention…

David punches a button on the remote.
ONSCREEN, popping up in the corner of the news,
a video-call with David's producer, JEFF HANCOCK (50).

Jeff is pale, nervous. He's in a busy TV control room.

                    JEFF
          -David-

                    SIR DAVID
          Are you watching the screen?
          Tell me what you see… I'm dying over here.

                    JEFF (nodding)
          Tell me about it….

                    SIR DAVID
          Who… can someone… let's get serious here…
          Are we now talking about a British version of the *Stasi?*
          Can someone become so delusional that they think they can
          rewrite our entire system?

 ONSCREEN, someone hands Jeff a script.

                    JEFF (distracted)
          No. What? Like…?

                    SIR DAVID
          It's impossible. What a load of bull.

                    JEFF
          Well… should we all quit right now?
          You know, retire to a nice villa in Spain…

                    SIR DAVID
          What do you think?

                    JEFF
          Tell the truth, I don't know.

                    SIR DAVID
          We're in the business of asking simple honest questions!
          We're not trolls.

                    JEFF
          If any attempt to 'talk back', leads to this…

The news report continues to cycle: "Prison Sentence For Abusers".

                    SIR DAVID
          -Lets move on-

                    JEFF (stressed)
          It's not going to be easy!

                    SIR DAVID
          -Don't worry-

                    JEFF (stressed)
          A little co-operation, that's all we need!

David looks at his reflection in the spoon.

                    SIR DAVID (into spoon)
          Not good. Look at me, I'm falling apart.

                    JEFF
          What do you want me to say?

                    SIR DAVID
          You think I should get a nose-job?

                    JEFF
          (under breath) *What next…*
          (to David) *You're rich, you're in the media…that's what happens…*

                    SIR DAVID
          Got the first one wrong. Incorrect answer.

                    JEFF
          …You're anxious, I can tell. Want to talk about it?

                    SIR DAVID
Yeah well, make yourself comfortable. (beat)
No, really, uh- let's talk about the uh, task in hand...

David pours another whiskey.

                    JEFF
Absolutely. Ready for the interview?

                    SIR DAVID
What about tonight's guest?

                    JEFF
...I got a big one. A really big one. Ready to go.

                    SIR DAVID
Don't humour me. I know it's been pretty dry out there.
The climate's not what it was.

                    JEFF
I hear that. Well... I have to ask (teasing)
whether we could use someone from the top tier...

                    SIR DAVID
Great, who we got?

                    JEFF
OK hold onto your pants a second...

                    SIR DAVID
How did—

                    JEFF
Yep, well...you'd be surprised.

                    SIR DAVID
Makes a change. Somebody worthy of my attention?
We could all do with a bit of a pick-up.

Knocks back his whiskey.

                    JEFF
Remember the risks. Don't be unprofessional—

SIR DAVID
—I'm not. But I can <u>be</u> however I want.

JEFF
You sound drunk.

SIR DAVID
No, no. I'm not that person anymore. Please…

JEFF
You're going to love this…

SIR DAVID
Talk to me. Please.

JEFF
Amanda… Barkham.

He's been waiting to hear that name a long time. David melts:

SIR DAVID
…You did it. I can't believe you did it.
There's nothing else you could do that…(lost for words)

JEFF
You've been waiting for this, I know.

SIR DAVID
Oh, you have no idea—

Blip! He ends the call. Jeff vanishes from the corner of the screen.

Amanda Barkham is still on the news.
David looks up at her image onscreen, straightens his tie.
A weight has been lifted off his shoulders.
He can almost start believing in his autobiography again.

SIR DAVID (to screen)
Thank you… Thank you for… this opportunity.
Finally, the public get what they deserve. After all…
(in his TV voice:)
"everybody loves a massacre".

MUSIC PLAYS: opening of Benny Goodman's *Sing Sing Sing.*

David launches into a dance number, black-bottom style.
He swats his tie back and forth, kicking out his heels. Big pelvic thrusts:

> SIR DAVID
> Oooh! Oooh!

He shakes his head back and forth, looking left, right, left, right…
He slaps himself repeatedly on top of the head, spins, drops back into his
chair—

MUSIC STOPS.

New scene: we are now in **SIR DAVID'S LIMOUSINE.**

ONSCREEN: the back window of David's car, moving through
lunchtime London traffic.
Sir David ignores the scenery. He's getting into character.

ONSCREEN, in the corner of his window, a pop-up box: "INCOMING
VIDEO CALL". Jeff appears in the box.

> JEFF
> *You're on the other side now.*

David triggers a second box ONSCREEN, next to Jeff. In it, a news
report: "Media Blackout Ends." Freedom TV is reporting on tonight's
interview: "Live Interview with Amanda Barkham Tonight; MP will be
guest on Heart of the Matter."

> JEFF
> *Don't worry you're not missing anything.*

> SIR DAVID (bored)
> Tsch. I don't know what I'm watching any more.

> JEFF
> *Come on Davey-boy. That's not the guy I know.*
> *And anyway, I thought you liked television.*

> SIR DAVID
> Like television? You can program them to serve
> every aspect of your life, but you cant get
> one original thought out of them. I don't know.
> How much do we actually know about these people?
> They're not too smart are they?

JEFF
Your audience tonight is going to see right through it.

Barkham appears onscreen, subtitled: "It is time to confront the media problem head-on…"

SIR DAVID
You can see, can't you?
What's the point in all this trouble?
If the scumbag wants to talk, we can talk!
If not, then just… shut up.

The scenery outside comes to a halt. David looks out the window.

SIR DAVID
I'm here.

New scene: **TV STUDIO.**

David sits in his presenter's chair, flipping through a script.
He wear a paper collar, smeared with makeup.

Amanda BARKHAM is pacing on the far side of the room.
She makes notes in a pocket-book.
She's young for an MP. Focussed, serious.
She's been heavily styled for the interview.

ONSCREEN: the opening credits for 'Heart of the Matter".
They pause half-way through and rewind back to the start.
Someone in the booth was testing the video.
The image switches to the pre-show countdown clock.

We're still an hour away from the live broadcast.
Sounds of the TV crew working in the background…

Barkham is trying to adjust her clip mic.

SIR DAVID (calling over)
So, do you know how to wear one of those?
It's quite straight-forward. I'll show you if you like.

Barkham ignores him. She goes back to making notes.

David interprets her silence as nerves. She's probably never been on live TV before. He feels sorry for her.

                    SIR DAVID
            You're doing the right thing, you know.
            Look, it's going to be painless, I promise.

Without looking round, she puts away her notebook.

                    SIR DAVID
            …What have you got there in your pocket?
            New legislation?

Barkham picks lint off her lapels. David gestures to the studio.

                    SIR DAVID
            You get to be the first guest of our new look!

ONSCREEN, the 'Heart of the Matter' title card: a revolving image of
Sir David looking serious.

                    SIR DAVID
            For you, this must be exciting! History awaits!

Beat. David gestures to the empty chair.

                    SIR DAVID
            Come on, you know what to do… please?
            This is… ah, head over! The floor… it'll be worn through
            with your bloody suffering…

Barkham sits down. She retrieves her notebook, takes more notes.

David watches her, waits for acknowledgement.

                    SIR DAVID (quietly agitated)
            I don't care. Drag it out, long as it takes.

Beat.

                    SIR DAVID
            Ms Barkham.

Long beat.

                    SIR DAVID
            Oh, you're deaf. Makes sense. It really does.

Long beat. David laughs.

> SIR DAVID (quietly)
> I'm going to break you. Just accept it.

He shuffles his question cards.

> SIR DAVID
> I'm not going to stop. Not until you're <u>done</u>.
> Not until I'm sure…

Barkham continues to make notes. David sours:

> SIR DAVID (quietly)
> You're dying to give me the boot. Well…
> get rid of that smile. After tonight,
> you're never going to stand again.
> Your own people are going to disown you.

David catches himself. He tries to dial back the anger.

> SIR DAVID (laughs)
> You've got nothing.
> Deep down inside, I think you know this.

Long beat. David breaks:

> SIR DAVID (snapping)
> God, I can't wait to see your face!
> Ms Barkham, if I even <u>think</u> you're lying, I'm just
> going to cut you from what's left of this show.
> (waiting for a response)
> Nothing?
> (re: the show)
> It'll be over before you know it.

Barkham doesn't look up. David waves his question cards:

> SIR DAVID
> I've made the whole thing so simplistic a dead cat could follow it.

Without looking up from her notes:

> BARKHAM (under breath)
> Oooo…

David twitches angrily.

> SIR DAVID
> Dead right, this is serious!

Getting in close:

> SIR DAVID
> I don't just 'disagree' with your policies,
> I want you <u>done</u>, OK? The people up in the booth
> —they've listened enough, they can tell you.
> I'd like to see you tried, considering the crimes I've heard.
> > (beat)
> I don't think you want this…
> Are you absolutely sure you want to challenge me?

David catches a look at her notepad. To his surprise, Barkham is simply transcribing everything he is saying. He laughs nervously.

> SIR DAVID
> I stand by everything. Everything I've said.
> Compare that to <u>your</u> speeches.
> Well, I think we can all agree, they're utterly meaningless.
> None of it means *anything*.
> There's no underlying message,
> no consistency, no through-line…
> > (gesturing to cameras)
> Oh, don't worry about it!
> It's too late for that! Shit happens…!

Barkham is still writing down his words.
He looks over her shoulder, adds some patronising advice:

> SIR DAVID
> Heads get a bit muddled…
> You might want to adopt shorter sentences,
> stop packing shit into your answers…
> I know when I'm being shafted, so don't waffle…

Barkham turns her pad away from David, keeps writing.

> SIR DAVID
> Hello? I'm not done!
> All these secrets… who gives a shit?
> This is a new side. An addition to your multiple personalities…

Losing his cool, face reddening:

> SIR DAVID
> Well, they're all getting shut down. It's <u>my show.</u>
> Just... don't panic when you think about
> all those screens of your poor face!
> Just... watch me as I... flush all this shit...
> out of our world!

Barkham turns.

> BARKHAM
> That actually made no sense. At all. What are you saying?

> SIR DAVID
> I—

> BARKHAM
> You think that *meaning* can just be brute-forced?
> There was no beginning, middle, or end there...

She traces around David's mouth.

> BARKHAM
> "Something" happened. But that's all you can really say—

> SIR DAVID
> —No. No. The truth is just too complicated
> for your little brain. I'll say it slowly so you understand—

ONSCREEN, Jeff calls through from the booth. Re: Barkham's clip-mic:

> JEFF
> *Ms Barkham— anything you want? Something doesn't fit?*

> SIR DAVID (to Jeff)
> Who cares? Sorry- that's life.

Jeff vanishes. Long beat.

David can't let the insults go. He needs to hurt her:

> SIR DAVID
> You think you're a hero, don't you?

                    BARKHAM
          I don't see the world in those terms

                    SIR DAVID
          This "story" of ours, it could be a movie, you think?
          Good versus evil… The climactic fight at the end…

Beat.

                    SIR DAVID
          It's hilarious how you act like you're un-easy with me.

                    BARKHAM
          Approaches are different.
          I don't see the world like you do.

                    SIR DAVID
          Yes, you said that already. It was shit the first time.
                    (shouting to his crew)
          Here, who wants a story?

David looks to Barkham for a response. She smiles.

                    BARKHAM
          Sure.

                    SIR DAVID
          It's about a unfit politician that tries to blame
          the media for her own incompetence…

Barkham softens. She puts away her notebook. Indulging his smugness:

                    BARKHAM
          Why not? I'm sure you could make it entertaining.
          You spin a good yarn.

                    SIR DAVID
          So?

                    BARKHAM
          Do you know… you're the only one
          I was willing to talk with? "You". Honestly.

Barkham leaning in.

                    BARKHAM
          My people don't need to know everything, but…
          I felt like I grew up with you. You were a hero of mine.

Beat.

                    SIR DAVID
          Very funny.

                    BARKHAM
          I'm not joking.

                    SIR DAVID
          Turn it off. These tricks are pretty cheap.
          You can afford better, surely.

                    BARKHAM (re: David's head)
          I'm curious… what's going on up in there?

                    SIR DAVID (on the back-foot)
          You looking for a new job?

Barkham shrugs. She switches her notebook for a makeup compact.

                    SIR DAVID
          You clearly need to perpetuate your unblemished
          image at all costs. This rich history of deception…
          must take strong foundation to cover that up.
          It's not cheap, is it?

David gets in close. He tries to catch her eye in the compact.

                    SIR DAVID
          I want to talk about your shameless attempts
          to suppress any opportunity for an open conversation.

No response.

                    SIR DAVID
          No? See, <u>this</u> is what we should be
          talking about tonight: hypocrisy.
          I mean: you've been busy, I'll give you that.

Barkham pockets her compact. Goes back to her notebook.

                    SIR DAVID
          This is clearly some kind of release valve for you.
          It's hard for you to stop.

David snatches Barkham's notebook. Barkham grabs it too.

                    BARKHAM
          Oi. Let go.

                    SIR DAVID (mock sad)
          Tears in my eyes!

David yanks the notebook out of Barkham's hands. He flicks through the
pages.

                    SIR DAVID
          Attempting to control this?
          Trying to hide this information from the press?

Barkham patiently holds out her hand.

                    BARKHAM
          I know you can't do that.
          Really, Sir David. I wasn't born yesterday.

David tosses back the book.

                    SIR DAVID
          Apparently.
          But you were, very recently, as I understand….

David moves off-set. He grabs a bottle of water from the craft table.

ONSCREEN, Jeff appears.
David's tone with Barkham has pushed Jeff close to a heart attack.
He speaks to David privately through his earpiece:

                    JEFF
          Are you feeling alright?

                    SIR DAVID
          -Hmm-

                    JEFF
          That… was… painful…

                SIR DAVID (shrugs)
-Mnnn-

                JEFF
Looks like she "passed"...?

                SIR DAVID
She was struggling from early on.
You could easily see her, no?

                JEFF
She should hate you, after all of that.

                SIR DAVID
No!

                JEFF
Despite the things you did—

                SIR DAVID
The woman isn't a human being.

                JEFF
Who can say?

                SIR DAVID
-I have no regret-

                JEFF
-Nevertheless-

                SIR DAVID
-She chose to accept-

                JEFF
But there— (sigh)
I take it back. She <u>loves</u> you. I'm sure of it.

                SIR DAVID
Come on....

                JEFF
Ready to explain the program to the people?

David is removing his make-up collar, distracted.

                    JEFF
Are you?

                    SIR DAVID (irritated)
          Yes!

                    JEFF
You say you're ready but you're not—

                    SIR DAVID (cutting him off)
          OK!

Jeff disappears. David turns to address the studio audience:

                    SIR DAVID
          People! How's it going?

Weak applause.

                    SIR DAVID
          Too affected. Again!

More applause.

                    SIR DAVID
          I know what you're thinking!
          "We need to understand how this all works!"
          It's very simple. First of all, give it up: Minister Barkham.

David gestures to his guest.
Barkham returns a well rehearsed smile. Audience applauds.

                    SIR DAVID
          A little bit too much, if you ask me.
          We don't want to see that!

ONSCREEN: the show backdrop (logo, Sir David's face) begins to glitch.
A hissing sound through the PA. A bad electrical connection?

David spots it— he clicks his fingers at the control booth….

                    SIR DAVID
          Power!

The show backdrop corrects itself.

David continues to talk to the audience…

> SIR DAVID
> Yes, everything is collapsing around us.…
> Nevertheless! We will tell you how to react this evening…
> The message is simple: just follow our lead
> and don't ask questions!

David laughs nervously. He changes tone. A quiet sincerity…

> SIR DAVID
> I know you've got anger inside you… I've heard you.
> Just wait until the time is right… Then go for it.
> This… is <u>your moment</u>.
> You want your five seconds of fame? OK!
> Throw whatever you need to throw…

David continues to talk with the studio audience…
Meanwhile, Jeff appears ONSCREEN again.
He whispers into the mic, face partially obscured.

Barkham touches her earpiece.

> JEFF
> *It's not easy trying to maintain a double life…*
> *All this plotting behind their back…*

> BARKHAM (to Jeff)
> Find someone else's shoulder.

> JEFF
> *Is there anything you want?*

> BARKHAM (to Jeff)
> No.

> JEFF
> *We're all ready.*
> *We don't think there's any suspicion of foul play.*

> BARKHAM (to Jeff)
> Good work.

Beat.

                    JEFF
          …Now you're going to come after me.

                    BARKHAM (to Jeff)
          Why?

                    JEFF
          Because you can.

                    BARKHAM (to Jeff)
          Pssch. You deserve a pat on the back for this.

                    JEFF (sarcastic)
          You believe that?

Barkham looks over to David on the other side of the set.
He's engaged in a series of ridiculous physical warm-ups.

                    BARKHAM (to Jeff)
          His world is shaking itself to pieces.
          The bits barely fit together.

                    JEFF
          …What do we do?

David approaches the interview desk again.

                    BARKHAM (to Jeff)
          Nothing, OK? And… here comes David.

                    JEFF
          This place is more than just a job, it's David's livelihood.
          Oh hell. All our livelihoods are under threat, aren't they?

                    BARKHAM (to Jeff)
          Well, that depends on your definition of being threatened.

Lights down. Long beat.

ONSCREEN: the countdown clock accelerates forwards.
We move to thirty seconds until broadcast.

Silhouetted, Barkham and David wait for their cue.

David shuffles in his seat. He looks over at Barkham defiantly.

She is completely still, serene.

David coughs to get her attention. No reaction.

David tries to mimic her professional pose, but his cough has tickled his chest, triggering a small coughing fit. He struggles to maintain composure.

Beat.

ONSCREEN: the opening credits of "Heart of the Matter".
Lights up on the studio set.

> SIR DAVID
> Tonight. We're here with Media Secretary Amanda Barkham—

> BARKHAM (interrupting)
> —Hello.

> SIR DAVID (stumbles)
> Ah… Minster. I wanted to challenge
> these… <u>insane</u> new hate-speech laws.

Sir David holds up a ring-bound document: a copy of Barkham's bill. He flicks through it aggressively.

> SIR DAVID
> There's no question, <u>we're</u> the target here.
> Anyone at home knows I am stating the obvious.
> How did it start, the—

> BARKHAM
> "complex affairs?"

> SIR DAVID
> ….that led you to <u>this</u> end? Was there much
> gnashing of teeth, a lot of vicious 'ins and outs'?

> BARKHAM
> -Well-

> SIR DAVID
> I'm sure there was. You cant pretend
> that there's no scandal here.

David throws down the binder.

BARKHAM
Where did you get that?
No, there was nothing of the sort.

SIR DAVID
When did the State begin its rapid decline?
Was it before or after you began to cheat the people here?

BARKHAM
Right-

SIR DAVID
Back to the start of these affairs…
I did some digging-

BARKHAM (cutting him off)
—Right, I'm sure you did your bit.
First of all, though, let me take…
Let me take an opportunity…
to really wish my sincere regrets regarding your late wife.
Is it too late to say, "I'm sorry?"

David tries to steer away quickly-

SIR DAVID
-Yes.-

BARKHAM
-I know you know this-

SIR DAVID
Before… things take a turn, perhaps, perhaps,
we should remember *why we're here.*

Aggressively tapping the ring-binder:

SIR DAVID
Before, you spoke about the importance of being honest.

BARKHAM
-Sir David-

SIR DAVID
I'm sorry, these attempts to control language…
they're utterly ridiculous. This kind of *repression* is…

                    BARKHAM
—Really, you can't talk like that.

                    SIR DAVID
No?

                    BARKHAM
No. It's just not justified.
I repealed our profanity laws, remember?
"God", "damn", "shit"…
            (looking into her camera)
"monkey bollocks", or what have you…

The audience laughs. David bristles at the bad language.

                    BARKHAM
…How I can be accused of censorship, I don't know.
I want people to express themselves openly.
Let it all out, that's what I always say.
Let people express their insides,
so we know who they really are.
…Now sadly though, this has exposed
the dirty underside of entertainment.

                    SIR DAVID
It's not—

                    BARKHAM
—Exceptionally ugly, exceptionally.
Lowest common denominator. Really.
You must agree, Sir David!

                    SIR DAVID
You turned television into this slum. How can you…
Now, you're going back in the other direction…!

                    BARKHAM
When an MP feels threatened, what else can we do?
We see a future where any kind of abuse… is finally past.

                    SIR DAVID (sarcastic)
Very inspirational. Where did you hear that?

                    BARKHAM
Time is always pushing us forward…

                    SIR DAVID
-Even if language itself appears to be moving backwards!

                    BARKHAM
No, my party has always been progressive.
We see what the future holds.

                    SIR DAVID
Against common sense, you appear to have made it
an offence to criticise politicians!

                    BARKHAM (correcting)
-to *threaten* politicians.

Barkham pours herself a glass of water.

                    BARKHAM
Sir David, what do you think is the point of news?

                    SIR DAVID
Uh-

                    BARKAM (teasing)
"Err"

                    SIR DAVID
Holding up… a mirror to the world.
So we can see who we really are.

                    BARKHAM (to audience)
So true! The man-

Barkham gestures, knocking over her glass of water.
The spill runs over David's lap, soaking it. He bolts up:

                    SIR DAVID
-Jesus-

Barkham tries to help, but David refuses.

                    SIR DAVID
-Just-

                    BARKHAM
OK…

David awkwardly scrubs his crotch with a handkerchief.
He gestures for the cameras to focus on Barkham, but still tries to keep
the interview going. Trying to think of a question:

> SIR DAVID
> Um…. Um…

> BARKHAM (into her camera)
> Moving on…

Barkham retrieves her makeup compact.

> BARKHAM
> You love this little trick. It's a classic.

She opens it. Shows the mirror to the camera:

> BARKHAM
> Here's a classic example of the thing
> you people <u>do</u>…

Looking back at David, ferociously scrubbing his crotch.

> BARKHAM
> Tsch. Behave yourself, Sir David!

Audience laughing. David stops, embarrassed.

Barkham shows David his reflection in the compact.

> BARKHAM
> Look at this. I mean, *really* look at it, yes?
> Who do you see?

> SIR DAVID
> Me.

> BARKHAM
> Who?

> SIR DAVID
> Sir David Bradley, the host of this programme.
> (Trying to resume the interview…)
> The way I see it, you have forgotten the
> fundamentals of how to be—

                    BARKHAM
—No you don't.

                    SIR DAVID (incredulous)
You don't believe I am who I say I am?
What are you trying to say?

Barkham holds the mirror closer.

                    BARKHAM
<u>This</u> is not Sir David Bradley. What happened?

The questions are meant to be clues.
She wants David to understand, but he just doesn't get it.

                    BARKHAM (exasperated)
This is sad! Incredibly weak.
          (re: the mirror)
Who is this?
          (giving up)
Your opposite! Everything is reversed!
Our opposite just looks identical to us.
Right, left… they're switched!

Re-pocketing her compact:

                    BARKHAM
It's easy to forget. Just like all opposing sides.
You need to be more careful with your words, David.

                    SIR DAVID
Right. More insane moral relativism from the ruling class.

                    BARKHAM
I don't believe in anything, including state control.
We both want the same thing: Balance! Justice! Symmetry!

The studio audience applauds.

                    BARKHAM (to audience)
You seem very much on my side.

                    SIR DAVID
They're just confused by your intentions.

                    BARKHAM
            With regards to this interview…
            I have a suggestion, if I may, Sir David?

                    SIR DAVID
            Well, I'd prefer you not to interrupt.

                    BARKHAM
            Again, I want to ask more questions. So many, in fact.
            I'd like to keep going. So… how about we switch chairs?

Barkham stands. Gesturing to her vacated seat:

                    BARKHAM
            You're just going to sit there…
            See how it feels to be on the other side for a change.

                    SIR DAVID (quietly)
            You're not going to co-operate, are you?
            You're going to keep doing this…

Barkham repeats her gesture. David tries to laugh it off:

                    SIR DAVID
            N-never.

                    BARKHAM (to David)
            Saw that coming. I think you can do better than that.

Barkham confidently addresses the audience.

                    BARKHAM
            OK! First example today!
            We've seen cynicism and misdirection
            instead of reporting the facts!
            Perhaps I'm naïve, but I still think you believe
            in freedom of speech, Sir David…!

Applause from the audience, encouraged by Barkham.

                    BARKHAM
            Well… why don't we make you
            an exciting new part of the show?

Applause from the audience gets louder, stronger.

50

Sir David smiles back at them, painfully. He's lost control and he knows it.

> BARKHAM (to David, re: audience reaction)
> I think that's the sign for us to move over, too.

Barkham leads the audience in a slow clap. It gets faster and faster....

> SIR DAVID
> Now?

> BARKHAM
> It's time.

The applause reaches rapture as David stands.
David makes it a pantomime. He plays along lamely, moving over into
Barkham's chair. Barkham takes the host's seat.

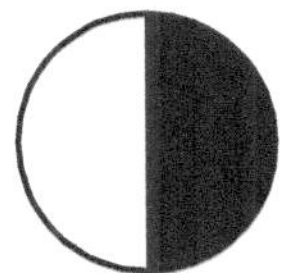

Barkham talks to camera, her voice now relaxed, smoother.

> BARKHAM
> It's time now, for us to move over
> to an exciting new part of the show...

ONSCREEN: Sir David's face and the show title have been replaced.
A new caption: "Hard Questions... with Amanda Barkham."

> BARKHAM (re: caption)
> —I think that's the sign...

David spots the caption. He shoots a confused look at the control booth.

> BARKHAM
> ...still think you believe in freedom of speech,
> Sir David? Well, why don't we make _you_ an example?

More applause from the audience. David twitches.

                    BARKHAM
          Today we've seen cynicism and misdirection instead
          of reporting the facts. Perhaps I'm naïve, but I
          never saw that coming. I think <u>you</u> can do better than that!

                    SIR DAVID
          OK, first-

David catches himself. No— he won't be drawn into this. He stays quiet.

                    BARKHAM
          You're not going to co-operate are you?
          You're going to keep doing this.

No response from David. He smiles icily, collar tightening.

                    SIR DAVID
          See how it feels to be on the other side for a change.

                    BARKHAM
          You're just going to sit there…

                    SIR DAVID
          So. How about we switch chairs again?

Barkham shakes her head, laughs.

                    BARKHAM
          I… want to ask more questions. So many, in fact.
          I'd like to keep going, Sir David—

                    SIR DAVID
          -Well-

                    BARKHAM
          —I'd prefer you not to interrupt.

The audience laughs. David looks around the studio. He'd worked with
these people for a long time. Some for decades. He has been betrayed.

                    BARKHAM
          I have a suggestion, if I may.
          <u>Your</u> intentions, with regards to this interview.
          They're just… confused.

                    BARKHAM (cont.)
You <u>seem</u> very much on my side.
We both want the same thing:
balance, justice, symmetry…

                    SIR DAVID (quietly)
-state control-

                    BARKHAM
I don't believe in anything, including a ruling class.

                    SIR DAVID
More insane moral relativism from the right…

                    BARKHAM
You need to be more careful with your words, David!
"Right", "left"… they're switched!
It's easy to forget. Just like all opposing sides…
Everything is reversed.
Our opposite just <u>looks</u> identical to us.
          (correcting herself)
"Your" opposite…

David twitches, arms folded. He looks smaller in this seat.
He's beginning to revert back into the depressive state we saw this
morning. Barkham observes the change.

                    BARKHAM
Who is this? This is sad! Incredibly weak!
This is not "Sir David Bradley." What happened?

                    SIR DAVID
What are you trying to say?
You don't believe I am who I say I am?

                    BARKHAM
No. <u>You</u> don't. The way I see it,
you have forgotten the fundamentals
of how to be "Sir David Bradley",
the host of this programme.

                    SIR DAVID
Who? Me?

                    BARKHAM
          Yes. How do you see yourself, Sir David?
          Look at this…

Barkham copies his defensive posture.

                    BARKHAM
          -I mean really, look at it! Well!
          Here's a classic example of the thing you people
          do— Behave!

David unfolds his arms. He self-consciously takes out his question cards,
taps them on the table:

                    SIR DAVID
          OK. Moving on…

Barkham copies his movement: taps cards of her own.

                    BARKHAM
          You love this little trick. It's a classic.

                    SIR DAVID (under breath)
          Jesus/ just—

                    BARKHAM
          /Just!

David and Barkham point at each other at exactly the same time.

Barkham laughs. The audience joins in.

Barkham has studied Sir David closely. She knows every gesture.

                    BARKHAM (laughing)
          So true! The man "holding up a mirror to the world.
          So we can see who we really are."

Barkham is suggesting that David was mirroring her, not the other way
around.

                    SIR DAVID
          Er-

        BARKHAM
"Uhh." Sir David…
what do you think is the point of news?
To threaten politicians? To criticise politicians?
An offence against common sense?
As you appear to have made it…

        SIR DAVID
-No-

Barkham is picking up speed. David struggles to get a word in:

        BARKHAM
My party has always been progressive.
We see what the future holds!
Even if language itself appears to be moving backwards…
Time is/ always pushing us forward.

        SIR DAVID (same time)
/"always pushing us forward."

        BARKHAM
Where did you hear that? Very inspirational.
        (resuming speech)
We see a future where any kind of abuse…
is finally passed back in the other direction!

        SIR DAVID
W-

        BARKHAM
When an MP feels threatened, what else can we do?

        SIR DAVID
I-

        BARKHAM
You must agree, Sir David!
You turned television into this slum…

David punches the desk. He won't be railroaded:

        SIR DAVID
How can you—!

BARKHAM (quietly)
—Now, you're going exceptionally ugly, exceptionally.
Lowest common denominator. Really.

David checks himself in his monitor. He is half-out of his seat, bearing down on Barkham. He looks intimidating, bullish.

Barkham gestures at his wet crotch. Coughs.

BARKHAM
Now sadly though, this has exposed
the dirty underside of "entertainment."

David sits down.

SIR DAVID
It's not-

BARKHAM
Let it all out, that's what I always say!

SIR DAVID
Ju—

BARKHAM
—Let people express their insides…

SIR DAVID
Pl—

BARKHAM
…so we know who they really are.

SIR DAVID
I—

BARKHAM
I want people to… express themselves… openly.

David gives up, sulks.

Barkham waits for him to respond.

Long beat. Eventually:

                    SIR DAVID
        I—

                    BARKHAM (interrupting)
        How I can be accused of censorship, I don't know!

                    SIR DAVID (under breath)
        God-damn…

                    BARKHAM (continuing list, loudly)
        …Shit….monkey bollocks… or what have you…

David spasms at the bad language on air.
Barkham is amused by his over-reaction:

                    BARKHAM
        I repealed our profanity laws, remember?

                    SIR DAVID
        -No! No! It's just not justified.

                    BARKHAM
        Really?

                    SIR DAVID
        You can't… talk like that!

                    BARKHAM (laughs)
        These attempts to *control* language…
        They're utterly ridiculous!
        This kind of *repression* is…

                    SIR DAVID (hearing 'repression')
        -I'm sorry?-

Barkham changes subject. She adjusts her angle for the camera. This is the
true purpose of her appearance here tonight…

                    BARKHAM
        Sir David, here you spoke about
        "the importance of being honest…
        before things *take a turn*." Perhaps.
        Perhaps we should remember why we're here…
        Before it's too late to say, "I'm sorry…"

Beat. Barkham looks for recognition.

                    BARKHAM
          Yes? I know you know this, regarding your late wife…

Barkham pulls a small remote control from her blazer.

                    BARKHAM
          Let me take an opportunity…
          to really wish my sincere regrets.

Barkham clicks the remote in her hand.

ONSCREEN: a photograph of a woman in a hospital bed.
David is posing next to her. Both offer weak smiles.
David is giving a thumbs up to the camera.

David sees the image. He immediately stands, removes his clip-mic.

                    SIR DAVID
          -Right-

He leaves the stage, heads towards the exit.

                    BARKHAM (shouting after him)
          I'm sure you "did your bit!"
          First of all though, let me take the people here
          right back to the start of these… "affairs".

Barkham pulls out an envelope. She removes a series of photographs.
David halts, quickly doubles back:

                    BARKHAM
          I did some digging…
          When did her state begin its rapid decline?
          Was it before or after you began to… cheat?

David marches back on set. He tries to block the camera.

                    SIR DAVID
          No. There was nothing of the sort.-

Barkham looks through the photographs.

                    BARKHAM
          Really?

                    SIR DAVID
          -Where did you get that?-

                    BARKHAM (ignoring him)
          ...Sure there was.
          You cant pretend that there's no scandal here.
          Was there much gnashing of teeth?
          Lots of vicious 'ins and outs'?

Barkham squints at one of the photos.

                    BARKHAM
          Well, I'm stating the obvious!
          How did it start, the complex affairs
          that led you to this end?

Barkham is perfectly composed.
David turns back to acknowledge the studio audience.
He stops blocking the camera, returns to his seat.

A moment to recompose himself. Then, to camera:

                    SIR DAVID
          Anyone at home knows I am the target here.
          I wanted to challenge these
          insane new hate speech laws...
          there's no question we're being threatened.
          Tonight, we're here with
          Media Secretary Amanda Barkham...

                    BARKHAM
          -Hello-

                    SIR DAVID
          ...Minster of Hell...

David laughs, then catches himself. Perhaps he is in hell?
He gestures to the rest of his crew.

                    SIR DAVID
          All... our livelihoods... are under threat, aren't they?

BARKHAM
Well, that depends on your definition of livelihood.

SIR DAVID
This place is more than just a job, it's-

BARKHAM
-David-

SIR DAVID (pained)
What did we do? Nothing. OK? And.. here comes-

BARKHAM
-David-

SIR DAVID (increasingly skittish)
This world… is falling to pieces.
The bits barely fit together. You believe
that you deserve a pat on the back for this?
"Good work!"
Now you're going to come after me— Why?
Because you can.
We don't think there's any "suspicion" of foul play!
We already know! Is there anything—

BARKHAM (calm)
You went behind her back.
Found… someone else's shoulder.
          (gestures to the photographs)
It's not easy trying to maintain a double life.
All this plotting…

SIR DAVID
OK. Throw whatever you need to throw.
You want your five seconds of fame? Go for it.
This is your moment.
Just wait… until the time is right, then—

BARKHAM
I know you've got anger inside you.

SIR DAVID
I've heard you this evening. The message is simple:
"Just follow our lead and don't ask questions.
Yes, everything is collapsing around us…

SIR DAVID (cont.)
...we will tell you how to react." ——See, *that's* power.
 A little bit too much, if you ask me.
We don't want to give it up, Minister Barkham.
It's very simple. First of all—

BARKHAM
I know what you're thinking...

David is sweating, disorientated. He ignores Barkham's prompts.
He taps the ring-binder.

SIR DAVID
We need to understand how this all works! OK?
People... how's it going to affect 'em?
Again, you say you're ready,
but you're not ready to explain the 'program'
to the people! Are you? Yes?

Barkham doesn't want to talk policy any more. She waits.

SIR DAVID (explodes)
Come on!

BARKHAM
She loved you. I'm sure of it.

Beat.

SIR DAVID
Take it back.

BARKHAM
...but there isn't a human being who can say,
"I have no regret".
Nevertheless... she chose to accept.
Despite the *things* you did. The *women*...

SIR DAVID
-No-

Barkham looks at the image on the wall:
David and his wife. The hospital. The weak smiles.

                    BARKHAM
          She <u>should</u> hate you, after all of that.

                    SIR DAVID
          No.

                    BARKHAM
          She was struggling from early on.
          You can easily see here...

Beat.

                    BARKHAM
          She passed very recently, as I understand.

David shoots her eyes of daggers.

                    BARKHAM
          Are you feeling alright?
          It was painful. I understand. But...
          you were yesterday, apparently,
          trying to hide this information from the press? No?

Barkham clicks her remote.

ONSCREEN: a newspaper headline, suggesting a new celebrity super-injunction. The article image is just a silhouette with a question mark, but now the identity is clear: David has been fighting to keep his sex-life out of the tabloids.

David looks at the screen, agape.

                    SIR DAVID
          You can't do that.

                    BARKHAM
          Really, Sir David.

Brandishing her remote:

                    BARKHAM
          I wasn't born attempting to control
          the tears in my eyes... I let go...

She clicks.

ONSCREEN, we see a shaky night-vision surveillance video. The film shows David approaching a terraced house. He's greeted at the door by a young girl.

Footage cuts to a recording through an upstairs window: David is cutting cocaine on a dresser. He paws the girl, now both in their underwear. Film cuts to the pair engaging in bondage. The young girl whips him viciously. David clings onto the window-frame, yelling instructions. Camera zooms in on his puffy face.

David is not enjoying the pain, but appears to be taking the whipping as a course of attrition. He desperately needs to be hurt, over and over again. He seems overwhelmed by self-hatred. (During the following exchange, the footage loops over and over:)

> BARKHAM
> This is clearly some kind of release valve for you.
> It's hard for you to stop! I mean…
> you've been busy, I'll give you that…

David tries to grab the remote from Barkham's hand, but Barkham skirts backwards. David winds himself against the edge of the table.

Barkham re-pockets the remote and photographs.

> BARKHAM
> Hypocrisy! See, this is what
> we should be talking about tonight!

> SIR DAVID
> No.

> BARKHAM
> "Any opportunity for an open conversation."
> I want to talk about your shameless attempts
> to suppress this rich history of deception.
> Must take strong foundations to cover that up.
> It's not cheap, is it? You clearly need to perpetuate
> your unblemished image at all costs…

David touches his earpiece. He shouts up at the control booth:

> SIR DAVID
> You looking for a new job?
> What's going on up in there?

> BARKHAM (re: girl on screen)
> I'm curious… these tricks are pretty cheap.
> You can afford better, surely?

> SIR DAVID (to control booth)
> Very funny, I'm not joking! Turn it off!

> BARKHAM
> I felt like I grew up with you!
> You were a hero of mine!
> I was willing to talk with <u>you</u> *honestly*…

> SIR DAVID (re: his audience)
> My people don't need to know everything-

> BARKHAM
> But why not?
> I'm sure you could make it entertaining.
> You spin a good yarn!

> SIR DAVID
> So do you.

> BARKHAM (firm)
> No. You're the only one here who wants a story.

> SIR DAVID
> Sure, It's about a unfit politician that tries to blame
> the media for her/ own incompetence.

> BARKHAM (chiming in)
> /"own incompetence".
> Yes you said that already. It was shit the first time.

David picks up his chair and throws it at the screen. It bounces off.

> BARKHAM
> Easy!

The screen continues to loop his dominatrix session over and over.
David's sad green face fills the back wall, flinching from the crack of the
whip.

David starts hammering on the screen, trying to smash it.
Barkham calmly rises.

                    BARKHAM
          With me, approaches are different.
          I don't see the world like you do.
          It's hilarious how you act like you're in a movie.
          You think: "good versus evil!"
          "The climactic fight at the end!"
          You think you're a hero, don't you?
          ....I don't see the world in those terms.

David gives up.

                    BARKHAM
          This 'story' of ours, it could be anything <u>you</u> want.
                    (gesturing to the screen)
          Something doesn't fit: who cares?
          That's "life"...

                    SIR DAVID (pleading)
          -Ms Barkham-

                    BARKHAM
          No. No. The truth is just too complicated
          for your little brain.
          I'll say it slowly so you understand...
                    (slowly)
          There is no Beginning, Middle, or End here...
          Some 'things' happen, but that's all you can really say.

                    SIR DAVID
          What are you saying?

                    BARKHAM
          You think that *meaning*
          can just be brute-forced out of a world
          that, in actuality, makes *no sense* at all.

Barkham believes that truth is relative, and that stories are constructions
that hide the true nature of the world: uncertain, infinite...

But David is not really listening.
He jumps up, shouts at the control booth again:

                    SIR DAVID
          All those screens! Off!

Barkham is disappointed. She wants him to understand…

                    BARKHAM
Your poor face…

                    SIR DAVID
Just watch me as I flush all this shit!

                    BARKHAM
-Well-

                    SIR DAVID
They're all getting shut down! It's _my_ show!

                    BARKHAM
Just… Don't panic when you think about all these secrets…
Who gives a shit? This is… a new side!
An addition to your multiple personalities…

                    SIR DAVID (to control both)
Hello? I'm not done until you answer!
I know when I'm being shafted… so… don't!
Waffle packing… shit-heads!

                    BARKHAM
-Got a bit muddled.
You might want to adopt shorter sentences…

                    SIR DAVID (to control both)
Stop!

                    BARKHAM (re: affairs)
Don't worry about it. It's too late for that.
Shit happens! There's no underlying message,
no consistency, no through-line.
None of _this_ means anything!

Barkham clicks her remote. The screens go black.
David sags, exhausted.

                    BARKHAM
Compare it to… your speeches.
Well, I think we can all agree,
they're utterly meaningless.

SIR DAVID (quietly)
Everything I've said, I stand by. Everything.

BARKHAM
Are you absolutely sure?

SIR DAVID
You want to challenge me? I'd like to see you try.

Barkham sighs. She expected better of him.

BARKHAM
-Er, considering the crimes I've heard,
I don't think you want this done…

Beat.

BARKHAM
OK… The people up in the booth-
they've listened enough. <u>They</u> can tell you….

Barkham nods to someone in the booth.

ONSCREEN: a photo of Sir David appears.
It looks like a news report.

We start to hear a recording of David's dialogue from earlier,
with subtitles appearing alongside his image onscreen.

All his sentences have been reversed- the cuts are prominent:

RECORDING OF SIR DAVID
I don't just disagree with your policies.
I want you dead. Right?

BARKHAM
This is serious.

RECORDING OF SIR DAVID
What's left of this show? Nothing!
It'll be over before you know it.
I've made the whole thing so simplistic
a dead cat could follow it….

David listens, baffled. He laughs at sheer stupidity of it all.

RECORDING OF SIR DAVID
Ms Barkham, if I even <u>*think*</u> *you're lying...*
I'm just... going... to cut you.
From deep... down... inside...
I think you know this.
God I can't wait to see your face...

His smile ices over.
Barkham stands behind him. She comforts him, hand on his shoulder.

BARKHAM (quietly)
Your own people are going to disown you.

RECORDING OF SIR DAVID
You've got nothing to give me.
The boot will get rid of that smile.
After tonight, you're never going to stand again...

The studio audience begin to boo.
The kangaroo court has reached its verdict.

BARKHAM (quietly)
Just accept it.

RECORDING OF SIR DAVID
I'm not going to stop. Not until you're done.
Not until I'm sure you're dying, Ms Barkham.
Oh, your death makes sense. It really does.

More jeers. David tries to pacify the crowd.

RECORDING OF SIR DAVID
I'm going to break your head over the floor.
It'll be worn through with your bloody suffering.
I don't care. Drag it out, long as it takes.....

SIR DAVID
-Please, this is-

BARKHAM
Come on. You know what to do.
New look for you! This must be exciting.
"History awaits!"

Barkham gently pulls David's suit jacket from his back.

David's shirt and tie fall away also. He stands in his white vest.
Barkham hands him back his jacket.

> BARKHAM
> You get to be the first guest of our new legislation.
> What have you got there in your pocket?

David reaches into his suit pocket: pulls out a pair of handcuffs.

> BARKHAM
> Look, it's going to be painless, I promise.

David slowly puts on the handcuffs.
Background chatter from the studio audience…

> BARKHAM
> You're doing the right thing, you know.

Barkham reveals a grey bag.
She gets close to his ear:

> BARKHAM
> So, do you know how to wear one of these?
> It's quite straight-forward. I'll show you if you like…

Barkham pulls the bag over David's head.
She pulls the drawstring tight around his neck.

Sound of approaching sirens.

New scene: David is now in the back of a **POLICE VAN.**

ONSCREEN: the back window of the police van, moving through
afternoon London traffic. It's exactly the same video we saw in David's
limo scene, now playing in reverse.

David sits in silence, hands cuffed, bag on head.

Barkham rides in the van with him. She now wears a full balaclava.
It makes for a strange combination with her professional pant-suit.

Unless perhaps it isn't Barkham? It could be someone else entirely:
the person that sometimes 'plays' as Amanda Barkham? Or perhaps
Amanda Barkham sometimes plays as this character.
Either way, she watches the road.

David coughs.

> BARKHAM
> …I'm here. Want to talk? We can talk.
> If not, then just shut u— You can see, can't you?!

Barkham waves her hand in front of David's bag.

> BARKHAM
> Tsch. What's the point in all this trouble
> if the scumbag is going to see right through it…

Beat. Barkham watches the window for a while.

> BARKHAM
> Your audience tonight…
> they're not too smart are they?

No response from David.

> BARKHAM
> How much do we actually know about these people?
> I don't know… you can program them
> to serve every aspect of your life,
> but you can't get one original thought out of them.

A thought occurs to her.

> BARKHAM
> Like television.

No response from David. She slowly removes his bag…

> BARKHAM
> Come on Davey Boy! That's not the guy I know.
> And anyway, I thought you liked television.

David recognises Jeff's words.

> SIR DAVID
> I don't know what I'm watching any more.

> BARKHAM
> Don't worry. You're not missing anything.
> You're on the other side now-

The back screen begins to glitch. London dissolves into a psychedelic corrupted signal.

Barkham drags David by his hair onto the floor.

The screen goes black.
We are now in **INTERROGATION CELL.**

Barkham tortures David.
Every move creates an echo of the dance scene from the first half.
David is painfully forced through his dance-moves backwards.
We hear a snarling reversed version of the song from before.

Barkham pulls David around by his hair.
Shew punches him in the face repeatedly: right, left, right, left…
Barkham puts him in a reverse headlock, knees him in the stomach.

> SIR DAVID
> Ooof! Ooof!

Barkham loops David's tie around his neck and throttles him.
He kicks and claws the air, gasping for breath.

Barkham releases him. He drops to the ground, wheezing.

Barkham moves to the table.
She unfolds a canvas hold-all of knives, inspects them.
She's upbeat, glad to be getting stuck in to some 'real work' for a change.

> BARKHAM (cheery)
> Everybody loves a massacre!
> The public get what they deserve, after all.

Barkham returns to David, kneels beside him.

> BARKHAM
> Thank you for this opportunity.
> Finally…

She rescinds the thought, instead just repeats:

> BARKHAM
> —thank you.

Barkham returns to her table.

BARKHAM
Oh, you have no idea…

SIR DAVID (out of breath)
You've been waiting for this.

BARKHAM
I know!

David begins to get up:

SIR DAVID
Theres nothing else you could do that—

Barkham turns, kicks David in the stomach.

SIR DAVID.
Ahh! You did it! I can't believe you did it…

SIR DAVID
Barkham. -*Amanda*- Please. Talk to me.

BARKHAM
You're going to love this.

SIR DAVID
Please.

Barkham pours a glass of something, drinks.

BARKHAM
No, no. I'm not that person anymore.

SIR DAVID
You sound drunk.

Barkham throws the rest of the glass in David's face.

BARKHAM
I'm not. But… I can <u>be</u> whoever I want.

David tries to crawl away.

BARKHAM (sighs)
Don't be unprofessional… Remember the risks…

Barkham pulls David back across the floor by the leg. She exposes his ankle, puts a knife against his achilles tendon.

> BARKHAM
> We could all do with a bit of a pick-up...

David mewls, struggles. Barkham holds him tight.

> BARKHAM
> Somebody worthy of my attention...
> makes a change. You'd be surprised...

ONSCREEN: incoming video call.
A young man appears. He looks like an IT administrator.
Behind him: a dark open-plan office. He's pulling the night shift.

> ADMIN DESK
> *-Yep-*

Barkham stops.

> BARKHAM (to screen)
> Well?

> SIR DAVID
> How di-

Barkham grabs David by the throat.

The admin assistant is typing. He gets up to retrieve a file binder.

> ADMIN DESK
> OK... *hold onto your pants a second.*

Returning to his desk:

> ADMIN DESK
> *Who we got?*

Barkham pulls David to his feet. She stands him in front of the screen.

> ADMIN DESK
> *Great. We could use someone from the top tier.*

BARKHAM (small-talk)
Weather? Well, I have to ask.

ADMIN DESK
I hear that. The climate's not what it was.
I know it's been <u>pretty</u> dry out there, huh?

BARKHAM
Don't humour me!

They share a laugh.

ADMIN DESK
Ready to go?

Barkham inspects a large knife from her collection.

BARKHAM
I got a big one. A really big one.

ADMIN DESK
What about tonight's guest?

BARKHAM
Ready for the interview.

David tries to regain composure:

SIR DAVID
…Absolutely. No, really, uh…
Let's talk about the uh…

ADMIN DESK
—Task in hand? Yes, well…
make yourself comfortable.

Barkham brings him a chair. David sits, facing the screen.
The video link is now over-laid with green text:

> D. BRADLEY
> DETAINED UNDER HATE SPEECH ACT
> THREAT TO MEMBER OF PARLIAMENT
> W/ INTENT TO HARM

> PRESS ANY KEY TO BEGIN TREATMENT

All questions from the Admin Desk will appear onscreen in this manner.

> ADMIN DESK
> *You're anxious, I can tell. Want to talk about it?*

David hesitates.

Barkham slams David's head into the table.

> ADMIN DESK
> Got the first one wrong. Incorrect answer.
> That's what happens.

> QUESTION 1: DO YOU WANT TO TALK ABOUT IT?
> INCORRECT ANSWER

> SIR DAVID
> Ww-hat?

> ADMIN DESK
> *Next: You're rich, you're in the media.*
> *…You think I should get a nose-job?*

> QUESTION 2: DO YOU THINK I SHOULD GET A NOSE JOB?

> SIR DAVID
> What do you want me to sa-

Barkham slams his head into the table.

> INCORRECT ANSWER

> ADMIN DESK
> *Not good. Look at me.*

> SIR DAVID
> I'm falling apart…

> ADMIN DESK
> *A little co-operation, that's all we need.*
> *Don't worry. Lets move on-*

> SIR DAVID
> It's not going to be easy
> if any attempt to 'talk back' leads to this-

> BARKHAM
Tell the truth.

> SIR DAVID
I don't know!

> ADMIN DESK
We're in the business of asking
simple honest questions. We're not trolls.
(consults next question)
Well. Should… we all quit right now?
You know, retire to a nice villa in Spain.
what do you think?

> QUESTION 3: SHOULD WE ALL RETIRE TO SPAIN?

> SIR DAVID
…No?

Barkham slams his head into the table.

> INCORRECT ANSWER

> BARKHAM
What? Like it's impossible? What a load of bull!

The admin consults the next question.

> ADMIN DESK
Can someone become so delusional
that they think they can rewrite our entire system?

> QUESTION 4: CAN SOMEONE BE SO DELUSIONAL THAT THEY THINK
THEY CAN REWRITE OUR ENTIRE SYSTEM?

> SIR DAVID
Who?

> BARKHAM (shouts)
Can someone!

Barkham slams his head into the table.

> INCORRECT ANSWER

The admin consults the next question.

> ADMIN DESK
> *Let's get serious here: are we now talking*
> *about a British version of the Stasi?*

> QUESTION 5: ARE WE NOW TALKING ABOUT A BRITISH VERSION OF
THE STASI?

Beat.

Barkham slams his head into the table.

> BARKHAM
> Tell me about it!

> INCORRECT ANSWER

> ADMIN DESK
> *Are you watching the screen? Tell me what you see…*

> SIR DAVID
> I'm dying over here…

Barkham holds David's head up so he can see the screen.

ONSCREEN: a photo of Sir David.

> SIR DAVID
> David.

Barkham slam his head into the table.

> INCORRECT ANSWER

> SIR DAVID
> No, no… This is too much… Oh please.

ONSCREEN: a photo of Amanda Barkham.

> ADMIN DESK
> *What's this? Little clue: you really want them to suffer.*

Beat.

ADMIN DESK (exasperated)
-My god-

Barkham slams his head into the table.

> INCORRECT ANSWER

ONSCREEN: a photo of some punk rockers from the 80s.

ADMIN DESK
What is going on?

SIR DAVID
I see… fucking… punks?

Barkham slams his head into the table.

> INCORRECT ANSWER

ONSCREEN: a photo of a horse.

SIR DAVID
…I see nothing.

ADMIN DESK
…Good.

Nothing happens.

> CORRECT ANSWER

ONSCREEN: a photo of a chicken.

SIR DAVID
I see nothing.

ADMIN DESK
…Bad.

Barkham slams his head into the table.

> INCORRECT ANSWER

ONSCREEN: a painting of Jesus.

                    SIR DAVID
          Jesus.

Barkham slams his head into the table.

> INCORRECT ANSWER

ONSCREEN: a drawing of the Michelin man.

                    SIR DAVID
          Fuck it… I see… one tired son of a bitch—

Barkham slams his head against the table, again and again.

> INCORRECT ANSWER
> INCORRECT ANSWER
> INCORRECT ANSWER

David's head remains flat against the table.

                    BARKHAM
          As if you don't get it! I know you do.
          You and me, we're supposed to work together.
          You act as if "day follows night", "lightning signals thunder…"
          You think you can just walk through a door,
          like it's the easiest thing in the world, come out the other side?
                    (shakes head)
          You can't see what's really going on…

                    ADMIN DESK
          It's sad.

                    BARKHAM
          Pathetic really.

                    ADMIN DESK
          Especially when they refuse to engage with you at all.

Barkham waves to the video-screen. The call ends.

                    BARKHAM (to David)
          As you might imagine… it's got harder
          to hold people to standards. I must say,
          they've got better at fighting back. Then we have this…

Barkham retrieves a hacksaw.
She holds the saw in front of David's eyes.

> BARKHAM
> …a clever "tool" introduced by our new government.
> Yes… times are changing. You never know what's coming.
> This is our job. Thats why were here.
> To help you see the world as it really is.

Barkham puts the saw behind David's ear.

> BARKHAM
> You want to know what's real? This.
> Exposing the truth. No need to thank me.

Barkham begins to saw.

Ten seconds blackout.

A small TV turns on.

Onscreen: a black and white image of Sir David, looking at the camera.

Caption: "A Party Political Broadcast from The Freedom Party. Presented by Sir David Bradley."

David's monologue has clearly been cut-up and re-assembled in the opposite order. The cuts are pronounced.

> SIR DAVID ON-SCREEN
> *Behind every injustice, there is always… a journalist.*
> *A terrifying, illiterate baby-kicking pornographer.*
> *These deranged homeless amateur hypnotists.*
> *Doctored photographs of "burning cities" financed by men*
> *who love to pleasure themselves with massive spanners. Look at them:*

TV screen shows courtroom footage from newspaper scandals.

> SIR DAVID V/O
> *All these reactionary, cum-stained pronouncements*
> *determined to terrify the public, who want Britain*
> *on the receiving end of their easily manipulated*
> *joyless excrement tunnels…*

Sir David smiling, superimposed over the Freedom Party logo.

SIR DAVID ON-SCREEN
The political system has finally been overthrown
by the right people… at the right time…

Vaguely patriotic stock footage: white cliffs of dover, police-men giving thumbs up, Churchill. Opening of Dire Straits 'The Walk of Life' plays.

Barkham's voice appears over footage of elderly people sat at computers, smiling at the camera.

BARKHAM V/O (reassuring)
That's us. Direct that anger towards us,
and we will show you the consequences.
We will not be intimidated. Trust me:
you don't know what this party is capable of…

Back to David. The image fizzes where footage has been re-spliced:

SIR DAVID ON-SCREEN
That's what I'm talking about! As a journalist,
I don't care about statistics, dubious spending, dangerous ideas…
My hands are full with the important stuff:
sexing up pop stars, dogs in sitcoms, whatever muppet
floats through the internet on any given morning.
Hot as I do it! That's my style!
I confess: I don't give a shit about information…
reaching a rational conclusion…

Image cuts to more surveillance footage of Sir David snorting cocaine.

SIR DAVID V/O
And sure, I'm smoking grassroots!
Thing is, part of being on this planet
is the right to ingest all the available shit.
Sometimes it makes you laugh!

Back to David talking to-camera.

SIR DAVID ON-SCREEN
You know, I'm so high that sometimes I forget journalism
is a decrepit old box of farts.
Once you've unpacked all their lies, it's hard not to make jokes,
when you challenge that 'quality journalism'.
Press, bright-eyed as ever, although…
these shiny little things are just for show.

Gesturing to his own eyes.

SIR DAVID ON-SCREEN
Look past them, you'll hear the sound
of the free press drowning…
Out: the lies.
In: the new world.
Bring celebrities!
The only real thing you have to pay attention to…
the cost of disagreeing.

Freeze-frame of Sir David's face. Overlaid logo for the Freedom Party.

BARKHAM V/O
The start of a new chapter…

Barkham enters. She turns off the TV.

BARKHAM
Oh God. It's so bloody over the top.

Barkham holds a breakfast tray: water and cereal.

We are now in a **PRISON CELL.** Light begins to return to the room.

Sir David is lying on the floor, hands cuffed in front of him.
His white vest is now stained with blood.
He has a bandage running under his chin, up over his ears and crown.
There is a bloodstain on the bandage where his left ear should be.
He looks dead.

Barkham puts down the tray. She looks at his body, concerned.

BARKHAM (playful)
This is… Sir David Bradley!
Host of Heart of the Matter!

No response from David.

BARKHAM
This is—

Barkham breaks off.
She lurches towards David- checks his pulse, distraught.
She rolls David into the recovery position, checks his tongue.

She slaps him on the back. No response.
Increasingly panicked, she slaps him again and again.

David coughs back to life.

Barkham slouches back, exhausted. She nearly lost him.
She holds his hand. Beat.

           BARKHAM
   This is all for you, you know. It's your fault.
   I wish you could see how things have changed.
   …Maybe when we meet in the next life.
       (beat)
   I know it wasn't easy in the end. For either of us.
   You might be surprised to learn: no, this isn't
   the first time I've done this.
   Some days it feels easier than others—

           SIR DAVID (interrupting)
   I need a drink.

Barkham fetches him a glass of water.

           BARKHAM
   See? I've been working hard. Are you proud of me?

He ignores the question, drinks thirstily.
Barkham helps David to his feet. She puts him in his chair.

           BARKHAM
   You've got to laugh!
   At least the place looks clean.
   Fixtures are in good nick.

Barkham turns the TV back on. ONSCREEN: the same adverts we saw
at the beginning, now playing in reverse order.

           BARKHAM
   …blessed with a TV that spews
   99% insurance adverts…

Beat. Barkham looks at David: hunched over, broken.
She can't leave him like this any longer.
Time to put him out of his misery.

Getting close to him:

                    BARKHAM
          I wonder… what you would think,
          if I said we were in your house, right now.

Sir David snorts.

                    BARKHAM
          What if! What if you were here… nice and warm…
          Your gorgeous townhouse:
          books on the wall, a meal on the table…

                    SIR DAVID
          I'm not.

                    BARKHAM
          I'm sure there's a way.
          How can you get back all the things you've lost?

                    SIR DAVID
          I can't. Is that what you want to hear?

                    BARKHAM
          I think you can. You can <u>choose</u> to believe
          any story you like. <u>You</u> get to decide.

Barkham moves around the cell, rearranging furniture.
She puts everything back just as it was in Sir David's house at the start.

                    BARKHAM
          …Act like today was just another day.
          Before, you came to work, did your job,
          then came straight home again.
                    (beat)
          Your home… or a prison.
          Which of those two feels more substantial to you?
          Maybe… none of this actually happened?

Sir David nods. He wants this to be true.

                    SIR DAVID
          Please.

Barkham unlocks his cuffs. Leaves them on the table.

84

                    BARKHAM
          Well. You did say please.

Beat.

                    SIR DAVID
          …Can I go?

                    BARKHAM
          It's your house! No one can tell you
          what to do in your own house!

She hands him a bag with his clothes in it. Sir David tries to dress.

                    BARKHAM
          The party is ready to make the call.
          When it came to a vote, I voted…
          We can't trust you to do the right thing.
          But… we can trust you to be yourself.
          Let me help you, won't you?

Barkham stands behind Sir David and helps him back into his suit.
He looks a mess, but dressed.

                    BARKHAM
          You see? Just take a look at yourself!
          There's no stopping now!
          It's coming back already!
          Everything is coming back.
          Jesus, who… is… this?!

                    SIR DAVID (dazed)
          Sir David Bradley.

Barkham puts the framed photo of David's wife back on the table.

                    BARKHAM
          That's right. He's ready. You're home, old boy.

Sir David sits. He notices the photo- holds it.
For a moment, he forgets everything else.

Barkham notices an advert onscreen. It's for a dating website: "Love.com"
Barkham turns up the volume on the TV set.

We hear the advert music:
an instrumental version of the opening song, 'I See You in Dreams'.

> BARKHAM
> Now this is what I'm talking about!
> I love this. I do. Genuinely love this song,
> I'm not ashamed to say!
> It reminds me how it feels to be completely… alone.
> It's so easy… anyone can apply their situation.

> SIR DAVID (dazed)
> It sounds strange. Not as I remember.
> Maybe it's a re-recorded vocal.

Sir David offers the handcuffs back to Barkham.

> BARKHAM
> You can keep them.
> They might be worth something someday.

David slips them back into his jacket pocket: the same place he found them earlier.

Barkham is swaying to the music. She's found David's karaoke mic.
David watches her.

> SIR DAVID
> Every word I said. Every threat, every promise.
> You managed to turn everything against me.
> (beat)
> …How did you even do such a thing?

> BARKHAM
> What are you talking about?
> There was no 'turning'…
> You just spent your whole life
> facing the wrong direction…

ONSCREEN: the advert dissolves into the karaoke video from the start.

This time, all the scenes play in the opposite order:
we see stock footage of a middle-aged couple, slowly becoming estranged.

They begin together, end alone, looking out to sea.

Sir David watches the footage, nervously. He find it upsetting.
This is not the story he wants to remember.
He wants to lose himself in the dream of love, not of loneliness.

> BARKHAM (sings)
> I learnt it all in dreams…
> I see you in dreams…
> I see you in dreams…
> I see you in dreams…
>
> You're all that remains
> (that's not what it seems)
>
> —My heart dissolves everything
> I learnt it all in dreams…
> I learnt a new routine…
>
> I had a song in my head
> I learnt that nothing ends
>
> Nothing really ever dies
> I learnt to live the same
> Wheels turning in the dark
>
> I taught myself to drive
> a guillotine right through my heart:
> I learnt how to survive
>
> All the clocks struck thirteen
> I learnt it all in dreams…

David cannot bear to listen any longer.
He takes a second mic and tries to steer the song in a different direction.

> SIR DAVID & BARKHAM (duet)
> I see you in dreams (I see you in dreams)
> I see you in dreams (I see you in dreams)
> I see you in dreams (I see you in dreams)
> You're all that remains (you're all that remains)
> That's not what it seems (thats not what it seems)

Barkham has been retreating throughout.
As they reach the last line, she gestures for Sir David to continue:

SIR DAVID & BARKHAM (duet)
My heart dissolves everything…

Barkham disappears.

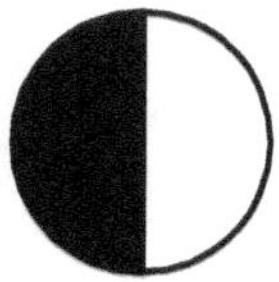

David continues to sing. As the song grows, his injuries retreat. A glow returns to his face. He is remembering meeting his wife, all over again.

SIR DAVID (sung)

…that's not what it seems.
You're all that remains.
—I see you in dreams.

I see you in dreams,
I see you in dreams,
I learnt it all in dreams…

All the clocks struck thirteen;
I learnt how to survive,
a guillotine right through my heart.

I taught myself to drive:
wheels turning in the dark.
I learnt to live the same.

Nothing ever really dies;
I learnt that nothing ends…
I had a song in my head
I learnt a new routine
I learnt it all in dreams.

My heart dissolves everything
thats not what it seems…

You're all that remains—
I see you in dreams (I see you in dreams)
I see you in dreams (I see you in dreams)
I see you in dreams (I see you in dreams)
I learnt it all in dreams…

Song ends.

Sir David tries to wipe a tear with his bandaged hand- he winces at the
pain. First from his bandaged hand, then again from his bandaged ear.

He looks around to get his bearings.
The stage has become **SIR DAVID'S TOWNHOUSE.**

Of course he is in his house.
Where else would he be at this time in the morning?
Any strange memories fade away.

David slumps back into his chair. Looks at his breakfast. A clock ticks.

David looks at the framed photo of a woman. Beat.
He guiltily drops the photo onto its face.

David begins to eat his breakfast, jabbing his remote control at the screen:

ONSCREEN: TV advert for "Love.com"

> ADVERT
> *Facing the wrong direction?*
> *You just spent your whole life-*

Bleep - he changes the channel. Now a driving school program:

> PROGRAMME
> Voice 1: *There was no turning!*
> Voice 2: *What are you talking about?*
> Voice 1: *How did you even do such a thing?*
> *You managed to turn-*

Bleep - he changes the channel. Now a dubbed French romance. Two
lovers, mid-clinch. (nb. It's from *Les Choses de la Vie*)

> FRENCH FILM
> Male: *….everything against me. Every word I said.*
> *Every threat. Every promise…*
> Female: *You can keep them! They might be worth*
> *something someday…*

ONSCREEN: the couple kiss.

Blackout.

PURE TEXT VERSION

1   My heart dissolves everything
2   That's not what it seems
3   You're all that remains
4   I see you in dreams (I see you in dreams)
5   I see you in dreams (I see you in dreams)
6   I see you in dreams (I see you in dreams)
7   I learnt it all in dreams…
8   All the clocks struck thirteen
9   I learnt how to survive
10 A guillotine right through my heart
11 I taught myself to drive
12 Wheels turning in the dark
13 I learnt to live the same
14 Nothing really ever dies
15 I learnt that nothing ends
16 I had a song in my head
17 I learnt a new routine
18 I learnt it all in dreams
19 —My heart dissolves everything…
20 thats not what it seems
21 You're all that remains.
22 I see you in dreams (I see you in dreams)
23 I see you in dreams (I see you in dreams)
24 I see you in dreams (I see you in dreams)
25 I learnt it all in dreams…
26 *—Facing the wrong direction?*
27 *You just spent your whole life-*
28 *—There was no turning!*
29 *What are you talking about?*
30 *How did you even do such a thing?*
31 *You managed to turn / —Everything against me!*
32 *Every word I said. Every threat. Every promise.*
33 *You can keep them. They might be worth something someday.*
34 Maybe it's the re-recorded vocal…
35 It sounds strange. Not as I remember.
36 *A loan! It's so easy! Anyone can apply! Their situation-*
37 I do genuinely love this advert. I'm not ashamed to say. It reminds me what it
        feels like to be completely
38 in love. / This!
39 Now this is what I'm talking about.
40 You're home old boy!
41 *—That's right. He's ready.*
42 *Sir David Bradley.*
43 *—Who is this?*
44 *Jesus!*
45 *It's coming back already. Everything is coming back.*
46 *You see? Just take a look at yourself. There's no stopping now!*
47 Let me help you, won't you?
48 *—We can trust you to be yourself;*
49 *to do the right thing… But*
50 *we can't trust you*
51 *when it comes to a vote. / "I voted!"*
52 *—The party is ready to make the call!*
53 *—It's your house. No one can tell you what to do in your own house…*

54   *—Can I go?*
55   *Say "please!"*
56   *You did*
57   *well!*
58   "Please."
59   *—None of this actually happened-*
60   *—Your home a prison? / —Which of those two feels more substantial to you? Maybe-*
61   *—You came to work, did your job, then came straight home again.*
62   *Today was just another day. Before…*
63   *—Act like*
64   *any story you like. You get to decide.*
65   *—You can choose to believe.*
66   *Is that what you want to hear? I think you can-*
67   I can't.
68   *—How can you get back all the things you've lost?*
69   *"I'm sure there's a way…."*
70   I'm not.
71   *—A meal on the table…*
72   *Books on the wall…*
73   *Your gorgeous townhouse..*
74   *all nice and warm…*
75   What if you were here,
76   in your house, right now.
77   I wonder what you would think, if I said we were
78   blessed with a TV that spews 99% insurance adverts.
79   You've got to laugh. At least the place looks clean. Fixtures are in good nick.
80   I've been working hard, too. Are you proud of me? Yeah.
81   I need a drink.
82   No, this isn't the first time I've done this. Some days it feels easier than others,
83   you might be surprised to learn.
84   …I know it wasn't easy in the end. For either of us.
85   I wish you could see how things have changed. Maybe when we meet in the
        next life…
86   This is all for you, you know. It's your fault.
87   This is…
88   This is Sir David Bradley, host of Heart of the Matter.
89   Oh God. It's so bloody over-the-top.
90   Start of a new chapter…
91   The cost of disagreeing
92   in the new world brings celebrity. The only real thing <u>you</u> have to pay
        attention to:
93   the sound of the free press drowning out the lies.
94   These shiny little things are just for show. Look past them, you'll hear
95   quality journalism. Press, bright-eyed as ever, although,
96   it's hard not to make jokes when you challenge that
97   decrepit old box of farts… once you've unpacked all their lies…
98   Shit, sometimes it makes you laugh. You know, I'm so high that sometimes I
        forget journalism is a
99   grassroots thing… is part of being on this planet… is the right to ingest all the
        available
100   information, reaching a rational conclusion. And sure I'm smoking
101   hot as I do it. That's my style! I confess: I don't give a shit about
102   pop stars, dogs in sitcoms, whatever muppet floats through the internet on any
        given morning…

103   My hands are full with the important stuff: sexing up
104   statistics, dubious spending, criminal mismanagement.
105   That's what I'm talking about. As a journalist, I don't care about
106   the consequences. We will not be intimidated, trust me. You don't know what
       this party is capable of?
107   Direct that anger towards us... and we will show you!
108   The right people at the right time, that's us.
109   The political system has finally been overthrown by
110   joyless excrement tunnels,
111   who want Britain on the receiving end of their easily manipulated
112   pronouncements. Determined to terrify the public!
113   Massive spanners! Look at them! All these reactionary, cum-stained
114   men who love to pleasure themselves with
115   doctored photographs of burning cities, financed by
116   amateur hypnotists...
117   this deranged homeless-
118   kicking pornographer...
119   a terrifying illiterate baby...
120   Behind every injustice, there is always a journalist,
121   exposing the truth. No need to thank me.
122   You want to know what's real? This...
123   this is our job. Thats why were here. To help you see the world as it really is.
124   Yes, times are changing. You never know what's coming.
125   I must say, they've got better at fighting back. Then we have this: a clever tool
       introduced by our "new government"
126   As you might imagine... it's got harder to hold people to standards.
127   Especially when they refuse to engage with you at all.
128   It's sad. Pathetic really.
129   You can't see what's really going on
130   the other side!
131   Come out!
132   Just walk through a door! Like, it's the easiest thing in the world!
133   You think you can?
134   As day follows night. Lightning signals thunder,
135   you and me, we're supposed to work together. You act
136   as if you don't get it- I know you do!
137   Fuck it. I see... one tired son of a bitch.
138   Jesus.
139   I see nothing bad...
140   I see nothing good...
141   I see... fucking punks
142   What is going on...
143   My god.
144   You really want them to suffer.
145   ...Little clue...
146   What's this?
147   Oh no! This is too much! Oh please.
148   *-David-*
149   Are you watching the screen? Tell me what you see... I'm dying over here.
150   *Tell me about it.*
151   Who... Can someone... Let's get serious here: are we now talking about a
       British version of the Stasi?
152   Can someone become so delusional that they think they can rewrite our entire
       system?

153   *No. What? Like?* / It's impossible. What a load of bull.
154   *Well, should we all quit right now? You know, retire to a nice villa in Spain?* / What do you think?
155   *Tell the truth, I don't know.* / We're in the business of asking simple honest questions. We're not trolls.
156   *If any attempt to 'talk back', leads to this…*
157   Lets move on. / *It's not going to be easy…*
158   Don't worry.
159   *A little co-operation, that's all we need.*
160   Not good. Look at me. I'm falling apart.
161   *What do you want me to say?*
162   You think I should get a nose-job?
163   *What? Next? You're rich, you're in the media.*
164   *That's what happens.*
165   Got the first one wrong. Incorrect answer.
166   *You're anxious, I can tell. Want to talk about it?*
167   *Yeah well, make yourself comfortable.*
168   No, really, uh- let's talk about the uh, task in hand.
169   *Absolutely.*
170   *Ready for the interview?*
171   What about tonight's guest?
172   *I… got a big one. A really big one.*
173   *Ready to go.*
174   Don't humour me.
175   I know it's been pretty dry out there.
176   The climate's not what it was.
177   *I hear that.*
178   *Well… I have to ask*
179   *whether*
180   *we could use someone from the top tier…*
181   …Great.
182   Who we got?
183   *OK hold onto your pants a second.*
184   How did-
185   *Yep, well…*
186   *You'd be surprised.*
187   Makes a change.
188   Somebody worthy of my attention?
189   We could all do with a bit of a pick-up.
190   *Remember the risks.*
191   *Don't be unprofessional.*
192   I'm not. <u>But</u> I can <u>be</u> however I want!
193   *You sound drunk.*
194   No, no. I'm not that person anymore.
195   -Please-
196   *You're going to love this.*
197   Talk to me
198   Please!
199   *Amanda…*
200   *…Barkham.*
201   Ahhh! You did it. I can't believe you did it.
202   There's nothing else you could do, that…
203   *You've been waiting for this, I know.*
204   Oh, you have no idea.

205	Thank you!
206	Thank you for this opportunity! Finally,
207	the public get what they deserve! After all,
208	Everybody loves a massacre.
209	** DAVID DANCES **
210	*You're on the other side now.*
211	*Don't worry you're not missing anything.*
212	I don't know what I'm watching any more.
213	*Come on Davey-boy. That's not the guy I know. And anyway, I thought you liked television.*
214	Like television?
215	You can program them to serve every aspect of your life, but you can't get one original thought out of them.
216	I don't know.
217	How much do we actually know about these people?
218	They're not too smart are they.
219	*Your audience tonight*
220	*is going to see right through it.*
221	You can see, can't you? What's the point in all this trouble? If the scumbag
222	wants to talk, we can talk! If not, then just… shut up.
223	I'm here.
224	So, do you know how to wear one of those? It's quite straight-forward. I'll show you if you like.
225	You're doing the right thing, you know.
226	Look, it's going to be painless, I promise!
227	…What have you got there in your pocket?
228	New legislation?
229	You get to be the first guest of our
230	new look! For you, this must be exciting! History awaits!
231	Come on, you know what to do!
232	Please? This is…
233	Ah, head over! The floor- it'll be worn through with your bloody suffering. I don't care. Drag it out, long as it takes!
234	Ms Barkham… Oh, you're deaf? Makes sense. It really does…/ I'm going to break you.
235	Just accept it. I'm not going to stop. Not until you're done. Not until I'm sure. You're dying
236	to give me the boot. Well, get rid of that smile. After tonight, you're never going to stand again.
237	Your own people are going to disown you! / You've got nothing.
238	Deep down inside, I think you know this. God I can't wait to see your face-
239	Ms Barkham, If I even <u>think</u> you're lying, I'm just going to cut you from
240	what's left of this show. Nothing? It'll be over before you know it. I've made it so simplistic a dead cat could follow it.
241	Dead right, this is serious.
242	I don't just "disagree" with your policies, I want you
243	done, OK? The people up in the booth- they've listened enough, they can tell you:
244	I'd like to see you tried, considering the crimes I've heard. / I don't think you want this.
245	Are you absolutely sure you want to challenge me?
246	I stand by everything.
247	Everything I've said!
248	Compare that to <u>your</u> speeches. Well, I think we can all agree, they're utterly meaningless.

249   None of it means anything.
250   There's no underlying message, no consistency, no through-line…
251   Don't worry about it. It's too late for that. Shit happens…
252   Heads get a bit muddled. You might want to adopt shorter sentences, stop
253   packing shit
254   into your answers: I know when I'm being shafted- so don't waffle.
255   Hello? I'm not done!
256   All these secrets… who gives a shit. / This is a new side. An addition to your
       multiple personalities.
257   Well, they're all getting shut down. It's my show. Just… don't panic when you
       think about
258   all those screens of your poor face. Just watch me as I flush all this shit
259   out of… our world! **That actually made no sense. At all.**
260   **What are you saying? You think that meaning can just be brute-forced?**
261   **There was no beginning, middle, or end there. "Something" happened.
       But that's all you can really say.**
262   No. No. The truth is just too complicated for your little brain. I'll say it slowly so
       you understand…
263   *Ms Barkham-*
264   *anything you want? Something doesn't fit?* / Who cares? Sorry- that's life.
265   You think you're a hero, don't you? / **I don't see the world in those terms.** /
       This "story" of ours, it could be
266   a movie, you think? Good versus evil… The climactic fight at the end…
267   It's hilarious how you act like you're un-
268   easy with me. / **Approaches are different. I don't see the world like you do.**
269   Yes you said that already. It was shit the first time.
270   Here, who wants a story? / **Sure.** / It's about a unfit politician that tries to
       blame the media for her own incompetence.
271   **Why not? I'm sure you could make it entertaining. You spin a good yarn.**
       / So? / **Do you know, you're the only one**
272   **I was willing to talk with? You. Honestly. My people don't need to
       know everything, but…**
273   **I felt like I grew up with you. You were a hero of mine.**
274   Very funny. / **I'm not joking.** / Turn it off.
275   These tricks are pretty cheap. You can afford better, surely.
276   **I'm curious…**
277   **What's going on up in there?**
278   You looking for a new job?
279   You clearly need to perpetuate your unblemished image at all costs.
280   This rich history of deception… must take strong foundation to cover that up.
       It's not cheap, is it?
281   I want to talk about your shameless attempts to suppress
282   any opportunity for an open conversation.
283   No?
284   See, this is what we should be talking about tonight:
285   Hypocrisy.
286   I mean: you've been busy, I'll give you that.
287   This is clearly some kind of release valve for you. It's hard for you to stop—
288   **Oi. Let go.**
289   Tears in my eyes!
290   Attempting to control this?
291   Trying to hide this information from the press? / **I know you can't do that.
       Really Sir David! I wasn't born**
292   **yesterday!** / Apparently.

293   But you were,

294   very recently, as I understand / *Are you feeling alright? That was painful. Looks like*

295   *she passed.*

296   She was struggling from early on. You could easily see her,

297   no?

298   *She should hate you, after all of that.*

299   No!

300   *Despite the things you did?* / The woman

301   isn't a human being. / *Who can say?* / I have no regret. / *Nevertheless.* / She chose to accept…

302   *But there-*

303   *I take it back*

304   *She <u>loves</u> you. I'm sure of it.*

305   Come on.…

306   *Ready to explain the program to the people? Are you?* / Yes.

307   *You say you're ready but you're not-*

308   OK! People! How's it going? Too affected. Again!

309   I know what you're thinking! "We need to understand how this all works!"

310   It's very simple. First of all-

311   Give it up! Minister Barkham!

312   A little bit too much, if you ask me. We don't want to

313   see that! / Power!

314   Yes, everything is collapsing around us. Nevertheless! We will tell you how to react

315   this evening. The message is simple: just follow our lead and don't ask questions.

316   I know you've got anger inside you! I've heard you!

317   Just wait until the time is right… Then

318   go for it. This is your moment.

319   You want your five seconds of fame?

320   OK! Throw whatever you need to throw…

321   *It's not easy trying to maintain a double life. All this plotting*

322   *behind their back.* / **Find someone else's shoulder.**

323   *Is there anything you want?*

324   **No**.

325   *We're all ready.*

326   *We don't think there's any suspicion of foul play.*

327   **Good work.** / *Now you're going to come after me.* / **Why?** / *Because you can.*

328   **You deserve a pat on the back for this.**

329   *You believe that?*

330   **His world is shaking itself to pieces. The bits barely fit together.**

331   *What do we do?* / **Nothing, OK? And… here comes David.**

332   *This place is more than just a job, it's David's*

333   *livelihood.*

334   *Oh hell. All our livelihoods are under threat, aren't they?* / **Well, that depends on your definition of**

335   **being threatened.** / Tonight, we're here with Media Secretary Amanda Barkham. / **Hello.** / Minster,

336   I wanted to challenge these insane new hate speech laws… there's no question, <u>we're</u>

337   the target here.

338   Anyone at home knows I am

339   stating the obvious. How did it start? The / **"complex affairs?"** / that led you to this end?

340   Was there much gnashing of teeth, lots of vicious 'ins and outs'? / **Well-** / I'm

341   sure there was. You can't pretend that there's no scandal here.
342   **Where did you get that?**
343   **No, there was nothing of the sort.**
344   When did the state begin its rapid decline? Was it before or after you began to cheat
345   the people here? / **Right-** / Back to the start of these affairs… I did some digging-
346   **Right, I'm sure you did your bit. First of all, though, let me take…**
347   **Let me take an opportunity… to really wish my sincere regrets**
348   **regarding your late wife.**
349   **Is it too late to say, "I'm sorry?"** / Yes- / **I know you know this-**
350   Before things take a turn, perhaps, perhaps, we should remember why we're here. Before,
351   you spoke about the importance of being honest.
352   **-Sir David-**
353   I'm sorry,
354   these attempts to control language- they're utterly ridiculous. This kind of repression is…
355   **Really, you can't talk like that.**
356   No? / **No. It's just not justified.**
357   **I repealed our profanity laws, remember?**
358   **"god", "damn", "shit", "monkey bollocks", or what have you…**
359   **How I can be accused of censorship, I don't know.**
360   **I want people to express themselves openly!**
361   **Let it all out, that's what I always say.**
362   **Let people express their insides, so we know who they <u>really</u> are.**
363   **Now sadly though, this has exposed the dirty underside of entertainment.** / It's not-
364   **Exceptionally ugly, exceptionally. Lowest common denominator. Really.**
365   **You must agree, Sir David!** / <u>You</u> turned television into this slum. How can you… Now, you're going
366   back in the other direction…? / **When an MP feels threatened, what else can we do?**
367   **We see a future where any kind of abuse… is finally past.**
368   Very inspirational.
369   Where did you hear that?
370   **Time is always pushing us forward…**
371   —Even if language itself appears to be moving backwards!
372   **No, my party has always been progressive. We see what the future holds.**
373   Against common sense, you appear to have made it
374   an offence
375   to criticise politicians!
376   **-to threaten politicians,**
377   **Sir David, what do you think is the point of news?**
378   Uh-
379   **"Err"**
380   Holding up a mirror to the world. So we can see who we really are.
381   **So true! The man-**
382   -Jesus!- / -Just-
383   **OK, moving on… You'll love this little trick. It's a classic.**
384   **Well. Here's a classic example of the thing you people do! Behave**
385   **yourself, Sir David! Look at this… I mean… really, look at it.**
386   **Yes… who do you see?**
387   Me.

388   Who?
389   Sir David Bradley, the host of this programme.
390   The way I see it, you have forgotten the fundamentals of how to be-
391   **-No you don't.**
392   You don't believe I am who I say I am?
393   What are you trying to say?
394   **<u>This</u> is not Sir David Bradley. What happened?**
395   **This is sad! Incredibly weak…!**
396   **Who is this?**
397   **Your opposite!**
398   **Everything is reversed! Our opposite just looks identical to us.**
399   **"Right", "left"… they're switched. It's easy to forget. Just like all opposing sides.**
400   **You need to be more careful with your words, David.**
401   Right,
402   more insane moral relativism from the
403   ruling class.
404   **I don't believe in anything, including**
405   **state control.**
406   **We both want the same thing: Balance! Justice! Symmetry!**
407   **You seem very much on my side…**
408   They're just confused
409   by your intentions. / **With regards to this interview…**
410   **I have a suggestion, if I may,**
411   **Sir David?** / Well, I'd prefer you not to interrupt.
412   **Again, I want to ask more questions. So many, in fact. I'd like to keep going.**
413   **So… how about we switch chairs?**
414   **You're just going to sit there…**
415   **See how it feels to be on the other side for a change.**
416   **You're not going to co-operate, are you? You're going to keep doing this.**
417   Never. / **I think you can do better than that. OK. First**
418   **example today. We've seen cynicism and misdirection instead of reporting the facts. Perhaps I'm naïve, but I**
419   **still think you believe in freedom of speech, Sir David… Well, why don't we make you an**
420   **exciting new part of the show? / I think that's the sign**
421   **for us to move over, too.**
422   Now?
423   **It's time.**

423   **It's time**
422   **now,**
421   **for us to move over to**
420   **an exciting new part of the show… I think that's the sign…**
419   **Still think you believe in freedom of speech, Sir David? Well, why don't we make <u>you</u> an**
418   **example? Today we've seen cynicism and misdirection instead of reporting the facts. Perhaps I'm naïve, but I**
417   **never saw that coming. I think <u>you</u> can do better than that.** / OK, first-

416   **You're not going to co-operate are you? You're going to keep doing this.**
415   See how it feels to be on the other side for a change.
414   **You're just going to sit there.**
413   So… how about we switch chairs
412   again? / **I want to ask more questions. So many, in fact. I'd like to keep going,**
411   **Sir David.** / Well- / **I'd prefer you not to interrupt.**
410   **I have a suggestion, if I may.**
409   **Your intentions, with regards to this interview**
408   **They're just… confused.**
407   **You seem very much on my side.**
406   **We both want the same thing: Balance! Justice! Symmetry!**
405   …State control…
404   **I don't believe in anything, including a**
403   **ruling class**
402   More insane moral relativism from the
401   right…
400   **You need to be more careful with your words, David:**
399   **"Right", "left"… they're switched. It's easy to forget. Just like all opposing sides.**
398   **Everything is reversed. Our opposite just looks identical to us.**
397   <u>Your</u> **opposite.**
396   **Who is this?**
395   **This is sad! Incredibly weak!**
394   **This is not "Sir David Bradley." What happened?**
393   What are you trying to say?
392   You don't believe I am who I say I am?
391   **No. <u>You</u> don't.**
390   **The way I see it, you have forgotten the fundamentals of how to be**
389   **"Sir David Bradley", the host of this programme.**
388   Who?
387   Me?
386   **Yes. How do you see**
385   **yourself, Sir David? / Look at this! I mean really, look at it!**
384   **Well! Here's a classic example of the thing you people do. Behave!**
383   OK. Moving on… **You love this little trick. It's a classic.**
382   -Jesus- / **-Just-**
381   **So true. The man**
380   **"holding up a mirror to the world. So we can see who we really are."**
379   Er-
378   **"Uhh".**
377   **Sir David, what do you think is the point of news?**
376   **To threaten politicians?**
375   **To criticise politicians?**
374   **An offence**
373   **against common sense? As you appear to have made it…**
372   No-/ **My party has always been progressive. We see what the future holds!**
371   **Even if language itself appears to be moving backwards…**
370   …Time is always pushing us forward.
369   **Where did you hear that?**
368   **Very inspirational.**
367   **We see a future where any kind of abuse… is finally passed**
366   **back in the other direction! When an MP feels threatened, what else can we do?**

365   **You must agree, Sir David! You turned television into this slum.** / How can you- / **Now, you're going**

364   **exceptionally ugly, exceptionally. Lowest common denominator. Really.**

363   **Now sadly though, this has exposed the dirty underside of entertainment.**/ It's not-

362   **Let it all out, that's what I always say.**

361   **Let people express their insides, so we know who they really are.**

360   **I want people to express themselves openly…**

359   **How I can be accused of censorship, I don't know!**

358   God-damn… / **"Shit", "monkey bollocks", or what have you…**

357   **I repealed our profanity laws, remember?**

356   No! No! It's just not justified.

355   **Really?** / You can't talk like that.

354   **These attempts to control language, they're utterly ridiculous. This kind of repression is…**

353   -I'm sorry?-

352   **Sir David,**

351   **you spoke about the importance of being honest**

350   **"before things take a turn". Perhaps. Perhaps we should remember why we're here… Before**

349   **it's too late to say, "I'm sorry." Yes? I know you know this**

348   **regarding your late wife…**

347   **Let me take an opportunity… to _really_ wish my sincere regrets.**

346   -Right- / **I'm sure you did your bit! First of all though, let me take**

345   **the people here right back to the start of these "affairs". I did some digging…**

344   **When did her state begin its rapid decline? Was it before or after you began to… cheat?**

343   -No, there was nothing of the sort.- / **Really?**

342   Where did you get that?

341   **Sure there was. You cant pretend that there's no scandal here.**

340   **Was there much gnashing of teeth? Lots of vicious 'ins and outs'? Well, I'm**

339   **stating the obvious! How did it start, the complex affairs that led you to this end?**

338   Anyone at home knows I am

337   the target here.

336   I wanted to challenge these insane new hate speech laws… there's no question we're

335   being threatened. Tonight, we're here with Media Secretary Amanda Barkham. / **Hello.** / Minster

334   of Hell. All our livelihoods are under threat, aren't they? / **Well, that depends on your definition of**

333   livelihood.

332   This place is more than just a job, it's- / **David-**

331   What did we do? Nothing. OK? And.. here comes / **-David-**

330   This world is falling to pieces. The bits barely fit together.

329   You believe that

328   you deserve a pat on the back for this?

327   "Good work!" Now you're going to come after me? Why? Because you can.

326   We don't _think_ there's any "suspicion" of foul play,

325   we already

324   know!

323   Is there anything- / **-You went**

322   **behind her back. Found someone else's shoulder.**
321   **It's not easy trying to maintain a double life. All this plotting…**
320   OK. Throw whatever you need to throw.
319   You want your five seconds of fame?
318   Go for it. This is your moment.
317   Just wait until the time is right, then-
316   **I know you've got anger inside you.** / I've heard you
315   this evening. The message is simple: "Just follow our lead and don't ask
       questions.
314   Yes, everything is collapsing around us! We will tell you how to react."
313   See, that's power.
312   A little bit too much, if you ask me. We don't want to
311   give it up, Minister Barkham!
310   It's very simple. First of all-
309   **I know what you're thinking.** / We need to understand how this all works!
308   OK? People… how's it going to affect 'em? Again,
307   you say you're ready… but you're not
306   ready to explain the program to the people! Are you? Yes?
305   Come on!
304   **She loved you. I'm sure of it**
303   -Take it back.
302   **But there**
301   **isn't a human being who can say "I have no regret". Nevertheless, she**
       chose to accept.
300   **Despite the things you did. The women…**
299   No.
298   **She should hate you, after all of that.**
297   No.
296   **She was struggling from early on. You can easily see here…**
295   **She passed,**
294   **very recently, as I understand.** / **Are you feeling alright? That was painful.**
       Looks like.
293   **But… you were**
292   **yesterday, apparently**
291   **trying to hide this information from the press? No?** / You can't do that. /
       Really, Sir David? I wasn't born
290   **attempting to control the**
289   **tears in my eyes.**
288   **I let go…**
287   **This is clearly some kind of release valve for you. It's hard for you to stop**
286   **I mean: you've been busy, I'll give you that-**
285   **Hypocrisy!**
284   **See, this is what we should be talking about tonight.**
283   No.
282   **"Any opportunity for an open conversation."**
281   **I want to talk about your shameless attempts to suppress**
280   **this rich history of deception. Must take strong foundations to cover that**
       up. It's not cheap, is it?
279   **You clearly need to perpetuate your unblemished image at all costs.**
278   You looking for a new job?
277   What's going on up in there?
276   **I'm curious…**
275   **These tricks are pretty cheap. You can afford better, surely?**
274   Very funny- I'm not joking- turn it off!

273   **I felt like I grew up with you! You were a hero of mine!**

272   **I was willing to talk with <u>you</u> honestly.** / My people don't need to   know everything- / **But**

271   **why not? I'm sure you could make it entertaining... You spin a good yarn.** / So do you. / **No. You're the only one**

270   **here who wants a story.** / Sure, It's about a unfit politician that tries to blame the media for her own incompetence.

269   **Yes you said that already. It was shit the first time.**

268   **Easy! / With me, approaches are different... I don't see the world like you do.**

267   **It's hilarious how you act like you're in**

266   **a movie. You think: "good versus evil!", "The climactic fight at the end!"**

265   **You think you're a hero, don't you? I don't see the world in those terms. This story of ours, it could be**

264   **anything <u>you</u> want. Something doesn't fit? Who cares? Sorry... that's 'life.'**

263   -Ms Barkham-

262   **No. No. The "truth" is just too complicated for your little brain. I'll say it slowly so you understand:**

261   **There is no beginning, middle, or end here. Some "things" happen, but that's all you can really say.**

260   What are you saying? / **You think that meaning can just be brute-forced**

259   **out of a world... that in actuality, makes no sense at all.**

258   All those screens! Off! / **Your poor face** / Just watch me as I flush all this shit!

257   -Well- / They're all getting shut down! It's <u>my</u> show! / **-Just... don't panic when you think about**

256   **all these secrets. Who gives a shit? This is... a new side! An addition to your multiple personalities.**

255   Hello? I'm not done

254   until you answer! I know when I'm being shafted... so don't! Waffle

253   packing shit

252   heads! / **Got a bit muddled. You might want to adopt shorter sentences** / Stop!

251   **Don't worry about it. It's too late for that. Shit happens.**

250   **There's no underlying message, no consistency, no through-line.**

249   **None of this means anything.**

248   **Compare it to... your speeches. Well, I think we can all agree, <u>they're</u> utterly meaningless.**

247   Everything I've said,

246   I stand by. Everything.

245   **Are you absolutely sure?** / You want to challenge me?

244   I'd like to see you try. / **-Er, considering the crimes I've heard, I don't think you want this**

243   **done. / OK... The people up in the booth- they've listened enough. <u>They</u> can tell you....**

242   *I don't just disagree with your policies. I want you*

241   *dead. Right?* / **This is serious.**

240   *What's left of this show? Nothing! It'll be over before you know it. I've made it so simplistic a dead cat could follow it.*

239   *Ms Barkham, if I even <u>think</u> you're lying... I'm just going to cut you... from*

238   *deep down inside... I think you know this. God I can't wait to see your face-*

237   **Your own people are going to disown you.** / *You've got nothing*

236   *to give me. The boot will get rid of that smile. After tonight, you're never going to stand again.*

235   **Just accept it.** / *I'm not going to stop. Not until you're done. Not until I'm sure you're*
        dying,
234   *Ms Barkham. Oh, your death makes sense. It really does. I'm going to break your*
233   *head over the floor. It'll be worn through with your bloody suffering. I don't care. Drag it out!*
        Long as it takes…
232   -Please, this is-
231   **Come on. You know what to do.**
230   **New look for you! This must be exciting. History awaits!**
229   **You get to be the first guest of our**
228   **new legislation.**
227   **What have you got there in your pocket?**
226   **Look! It's going to be painless, I promise.**
225   **You're doing the right thing, you know.**
224   **So, do you know how to wear one of these? It's quite straight-forward. I'll**
        show you if you like.
223   **…I'm here.**
222   **Want to talk? We can talk. If not, then just shut up—**
221   **You can see, can't you? What's the point in all this trouble if the scumbag**
220   **is going to see right through it…**
219   **Your audience tonight…**
218   **They're not too smart are they?**
217   **How much do we actually know about these people?**
216   **I don't know…**
215   **You can program them to serve every aspect of your life, but you cant get**
        one original thought out of them.
214   **…Like television.**
213   **Come on Davey Boy. That's not the guy I know. And anyway, I thought**
        you liked television.
212   I don't know what I'm watching any more.
211   **Don't worry. You're not missing anything.**
210   **You're on the other side now-**
209   ** DAVID IS BEATEN **
208   **Everybody loves a massacre.**
207   **The public get what they deserve after all!**
206   **Thank you for this opportunity! Finally,**
205   **Thank you!**
204   **Oh, you have no idea.**
203   You've been waiting for this / **I know!**
202   Theres nothing else you could do that-
201   Ahh! Ah ah! You did it. I can't believe you did it…
200   Barkham.
199   *-Amanda-*
198   Please.
197   Talk to me.
196   **You're going to love this.**
195   **Please.**
194   **No, no. I'm not that person anymore.**
193   You sound drunk.
192   **I'm not. But… I can be whoever I want.**
191   **Don't be unprofessional.**
190   **Remember the risks.**
189   **We could all do with a bit of a pick-up.**
188   **Somebody worthy of my attention**
187   **makes a change.**

186   **You'd be surprised.**
185   *Yep.* / **Well?**
184   How did-
183   *OK… hold onto your pants a second.*
182   *Who we got?*
181   *Great.*
180   *We could use someone from the top tier.*
179   **Weather?**
178   **Well, I have to ask.**
177   *I hear that.*
176   *The climate's not what it was.*
175   *I know it's been <u>pretty</u> dry out there, huh?*
174   **Don't humour me.**
173   *Ready to go?*
172   **I got a big one. A really big one.**
171   *What about tonight's guest?*
170   **Ready for the interview.**
169   …Absolutely.
168   No, really, uh. let's talk about the uh… / *"Task in hand?"*
167   *Yes, well, make yourself comfortable.*
166   *You're anxious, I can tell. Want to talk about it?*
165   *Got the first one wrong. Incorrect answer.*
164   *That's what happens.*
163   What? / *Next: You're rich, you're in the media.*
162   *…You think I should get a nose-job?*
161   What do you want me to say-
160   *Not good. Look at me.* / I'm falling apart…
159   *A little co-operation, that's all we need.*
158   *Don't worry.*
157   *Lets move on-* / It's not going to be easy
156   if any attempt to 'talk back' leads to this.
155   **Tell the truth.** / I don't know! / *We're in the business of asking simple honest questions. We're not trolls.*
154   *Well… "Should we all quit right now?" You know, retire to a nice villa in Spain? What do you think?*
153   …no? / **What? Like it's impossible? What a load of bull!**
152   *Can someone become so delusional that they think they can rewrite our entire system?*
151   Who? / **Can someone!** / *Let's get serious here: are we now talking about a British version of the Stasi?*
150   **Tell me about it!**
149   *Are you watching the screen? Tell me what you see…* / I'm dying over here
148   David.
147   No, no… This is too much… Oh please.
146   *What's this?*
145   *Little clue:*
144   *You really want them to suffer.*
143   *-My god-*
142   *What is going on?*
141   I see… fucking… punks.
140   I see nothing. / *Good.*
139   I see nothing. / *Bad.*
138   Jesus…
137   Fuck it. I see one tired son of a bitch.
136   **As if you don't get it! I know you do.**

135   You and me, we're supposed to work together. You act
134   as if day follows night, lightning signals thunder…
133   You think you can
132   just walk through a door, like it's the easiest thing in the world,
131   come out
130   the other side?
129   You can't see what's really going on.
128   *It's sad.* / **Pathetic really.**
127   *Especially when they refuse to engage with you at all.*
126   **As you might imagine…. it's got harder to hold people to standards.**
125   **I must say, they've got better at fighting back. Then we have this… a
        clever tool introduced by our new government.**
124   **Yes… times are changing. You never know what's coming.**
123   **This is __our__ job. Thats why were here. To help you see the world as it
        really is.**
122   **You want to know what's real? This.**
121   **Exposing the truth. No need to thank me.**
120   *Behind every injustice, there is always… a journalist.*
119   *A terrifying, illiterate baby-*
118   *kicking pornographer.*
117   *These deranged homeless*
116   *amateur hypnotists.*
115   *Doctored photographs of burning cities financed by*
114   *men who love to pleasure themselves with*
113   *massive spanners. Look at them: all these reactionary, cum-stained*
112   *pronouncements, determined to terrify the public,*
111   *who want Britain on the receiving end of their easily manipulated*
110   *joyless excrement tunnels.*
109   *The political system has finally been overthrown by*
108   *the right people at the right time.* / **That's us.**
107   **Direct that anger towards us, and we will show you**
106   **the consequences. We will not be intimidated. Trust me: you don't know
        what this party is capable of.**
105   *That's what I'm talking about! As a journalist, I don't care about*
104   *statistics, dubious spending, dangerous ideas.*
103   *My hands are full with the important stuff: sexing up*
102   *pop stars, dogs in sitcoms, whatever muppet floats through the internet on any given morning.*
101   *Hot as I do it! That's my style. I confess: I don't give a shit about*
100   *information, reaching a rational conclusion. And sure, I'm smoking*
99   *grassroots! Thing is, part of being on this planet is the right to ingest all the available*
98   *shit. Sometimes it makes you laugh. You know, I'm so high that sometimes I forget journalism
        is a*
97   *decrepit old box of farts. Once you've unpacked all their lies,*
96   *it's hard not to make jokes, when you challenge that*
95   *'quality journalism'. Press, bright-eyed as ever, although*
94   *These shiny little things are just for show. Look past them, you'll hear*
93   *the sound of the free press drowning. Out: the lies.*
92   *In: the new world. Bring celebrities. The only real thing __you__ have to pay attention to--*
91   *the cost of disagreeing.*
90   *…The start of a new chapter.*
89   **Oh God. It's so bloody over the top.**
88   **This is Sir David Bradley, host of Heart of the Matter.**
87   **This is…**
86   **This is all for you, you know. It's your fault.**

85	I wish you could see how things have changed. Maybe when we meet in the next life.
84	I know it wasn't easy in the end. For either of us.
83	You might be surprised to learn,
82	No, this isn't the first time I've done this. Some days it feels easier than others.
81	I need a drink.
80	See? I've been working hard. Are you proud of me? / Yes.
79	You've got to laugh. At least the place looks clean. Fixtures are in good nick.
78	…blessed with a TV that spews 99% insurance adverts.
77	I wonder what you would think, if I said we were
76	In your house, right now.
75	What if you were here,
74	nice and warm
73	Your gorgeous townhouse
72	Books on the wall.
71	a meal on the table…
70	I'm not.
69	I'm sure there's a way.
68	How can you get back all the things you've lost?
67	I can't,
66	is that what you want to hear? / I think you can.
65	You can choose to believe
64	any story you like. You get to decide.
63	Act like
62	today was just another day. Before,
61	you came to work, did your job, then came straight home again.
60	Your home or a prison. Which of those two feels more substantial to you? Maybe
59	none of this actually happened.
58	Please.
57	Well.
56	You did
55	say please.
54	Can I go?
53	It's your house. No one can tell you what to do in your own house.
52	The party is ready to make the call.
51	When it came to a vote, I voted…
50	We can't trust you
49	to do the right thing. But…
48	we can trust you to be yourself.
47	Let me help you, won't you?
46	You see? Just take a look at yourself. There's no stopping now!
45	It's coming back already. Everything is coming back.
44	Jesus,
43	who… is… this?!
42	Sir David Bradley.
41	That's right. He's ready.
40	You're home, old boy.
39	Now this is what I'm talking about!
38	I love this.
37	I do. Genuinely love this advert. I'm not ashamed to say. It reminds me what it feels like to be completely

36	**alone. It's so easy- anyone can apply their situation.**
35	It sounds strange. Not as I remember.
34	Maybe it's a re-recorded vocal.
33	**You can keep them. They might be worth something someday.**
32	Every word I said. Every threat. Every promise.
31	You managed to turn everything against me.
30	…How did you even do such a thing?
29	**What are you talking about?**
28	**There was no… "turning"…**
27	**You just spent your whole life**
26	**facing the wrong direction…**
25	**I learnt it all in dreams**
24	**I see you in dreams**
23	**I see you in dreams**
22	**I see you in dreams**
21	**You're all that remains**
20	**thats not what it seems**
19	**—My heart dissolves everything**
18	**I learnt it all in dreams**
17	**I learnt a new routine…**
16	**I had a song in my head**
15	**I learnt that nothing ends**
14	**Nothing really ever dies**
13	**I learnt to live the same**
12	**Wheels turning in the dark**
11	**I taught myself to drive**
10	**A guillotine right through my heart**
9	**I learnt how to survive**
8	**All the clocks struck thirteen**
7	**I learnt it all in dreams**
6	**I see you in dreams (I see you in dreams)**
5	**I see you in dreams (I see you in dreams)**
4	**I see you in dreams (I see you in dreams)**
3	**you're all that remains (you're all that remains)**
2	**that's not what it seems (thats not what it seems)**
1	**My heart dissolves everything…**

1	My heart dissolves everything
2	That's not what it seems
3	You're all that remains
4	I see you in dreams (I see you in dreams)
5	I see you in dreams (I see you in dreams)
6	I see you in dreams (I see you in dreams)
7	I learnt it all in dreams…
8	All the clocks struck thirteen
9	I learnt how to survive
10	A guillotine right through my heart
11	I taught myself to drive
12	Wheels turning in the dark

13   I learnt to live the same
14   Nothing really ever dies
15   I learnt that nothing ends
16   I had a song in my head
17   I learnt a new routine
18   I learnt it all in dreams
19   —My heart dissolves everything
20   thats not what it seems
21   You're all that remains
22   I see you in dreams (I see you in dreams)
23   I see you in dreams (I see you in dreams)
24   I see you in dreams (I see you in dreams)
25   I learnt it all in dreams…
26   *—Facing the wrong direction?*
27   *You just spent your whole life-*
28   *—There was no turning!*
29   *What are you talking about?*
30   *How did you even do such a thing?*
31   *You managed to turn / —Everything against me!*
32   *Every word I said. Every threat. Every promise.*
33   *You can keep them. They might be worth something someday—*

PARTY TRAP

September 13th to October 1st 2016
Shoreditch Town Hall

Written by Ross Sutherland
Directed by Rob Watt

Sir David Bradley............ Simon Hepworth
Amanda Barkham................. Zara Plessard
Jeff Hancock............... Michael Warburton
Admin Desk........................ Ian Attard

Original music by Jeremy Warmsley
with additional vocals by Elizabeth Sankey

Stage design: Rob Watt
Lighting design and stage management: Tom Clutterbuck
Lighting associate: Lucy Adams
Fight choreography: Jonathan Holby

Produced by Show + Tell
Commissioned and supported by Shoreditch Town Hall
and Arts Council England.

Additional video work:
Tamara Saffir, Aspen Reiss, Alice Bell, Amanda Reed, Angus Dunican,
Audrey Brown, Benjamin Murray, Edward Wolstenholme, Guy Morgan,
Jan Shepherd, Jo Ashe, John Conway, Luisa Guerreiro, Mark Niel,
Olivette Cole-Wilson, Orla Jackson, Pip Mayo, Robin Miller,
Sara Wingate Gray, Alexa Hartley, Cassie Bradley, Emily Keller,
Sean Pogmore, Owen Jenkins, Laura Lawless, Robert Sladden,
Nick Edison.

Thanks to our supporters:
Alex Bird, Drew Taylor, Clare Currie, Natalie Jones, Martin Figura,
Vanessa Kisuule, Polly Wright, Charlie Miller, Lauren Hurst,
Emma Hammond, Caroline Lazar, Jake Campbell, Charlie Lyne,
Andy Craven-Griffiths, Hannah Barry, David Hanson, Kieran Hurley,
Megan Vaughan, Chris Stewart, Crystal Bennes, Jack Satchell,
Helen Jewell, Emily Philippou, Alice Bell, Peter Howell,
Chloe Walker Harrison, Callum Mitchell, Andy Bennet,
Owen Craven-Griffiths, Emily Dening, Paul Rowland, Julien Matthews,
Doug Kerr, Will Lakeman, Suzanne Hardy, AF Harrold, John Osborne.

www.ingramcontent.com/pod-product-compliance
Lightning Source LLC
Chambersburg PA
CBHW031312060726
47590CB00003B/1177